WE STAND AGAINST EVIL

Praxos Academy

SG TURNER

We Stand Against Evil

Praxos Academy
by SG Turner

Published by Chill Out Press

For more information about the author SG Turner and upcoming books, please visit

www.chilloutpress.com/sgturner

'I've just got this horrible feeling that we're travelling to the wrong place,' sighed Lana rather too loudly as she gazed out of the aeroplane's window, seeing nothing but thick, fluffy clouds beneath them and blue sky above.

'Eleanor told me she was in Canada, Sis. She's not usually wrong,' Emma said, fidgeting with her long dark hair.

'Yeah I know,' she replied quietly, sitting back in the seat before continuing, 'But I just have this really weird feeling deep in my stomach and these kinds of feelings aren't normally wrong. Are they?'

'I guess not. Look, just go and tell Declan,' Emma muttered under her breath before closing her eyes and turning away from her sister.

'Are you alright, Emma?' Lana asked.

'Yeah, why wouldn't I be?' she answered with her eyes still closed.

'You're just not yourself, you know?'

'Yeah, whatever, I'm going to sleep. Go and talk to Declan.'

Lana raised her eyebrows and fumbled with her seatbelt, eventually undoing it. Standing up, she scanned the seats around her until she spotted Declan who was talking quietly to Aria and Marlene.

'Hey Lana,' Aria smiled. 'Are you okay?'

Nodding, Lana leaned against the seat, 'A bit worried about Emma though.'

'What do you mean?' asked Declan as they all glanced over to look at her sister.

'She's not herself. I mean really not herself. She sounds more like me and that's never a good thing, is it?'

Declan raised his eyebrows, 'She'll be okay. She's still adjusting to what happened. It's not easy getting over killing someone,' Declan added in a whisper, glancing around at the strangers surrounding them.

Marlene nodded, grimacing slightly as she continued to watch the goth girl in the seat up ahead of them. 'Would you like me to talk to her?'

'She said she's going to sleep, but maybe later?'

Marlene nodded.

'There's something else though,' Lana added.

'What's up?' Declan asked, concerned.

'I just keep getting this feeling that we're going to the wrong place.'

'What do you mean? One of your gifted feelings?'

Lana nodded.

'You don't think Eleanor is in Canada?' Aria asked.

'I'm not sure. I just have this weird feeling about Scotland.'

'Scotland?' Declan said loudly. 'That's weird. Eleanor definitely said Canada.'

'I know, which is why I'm so confused. My feelings are usually right. I don't get it.'

'Well, we're flying to Calgary right now, there's not much we can do to change that.'

Lana nodded and sighed, 'I don't understand why we couldn't have used the private jet again and then we could have just turned it around.'

Declan dropped his head to one side, 'We've already talked about this Lana. Eleanor left strict instructions about what we should do in the event of anything happening to her, especially when it concerns the Skulls. We have to keep things under the radar which means we have no choice but to use limited resources.

We don't know how much Madge knows so by flying economy under false aliases, we've got a better chance of finding her.'

'Not if we're flying to the wrong country,' Lana exclaimed, crossing her arms like a naughty child.

'Look, I know you're angry about so many things but we have to do this properly. It's what Eleanor wanted.'

'What? That all of our friends should stay in England?'

'Oh c'mon, Lana. We've been over this too. Most of the Watchers in your class were not given permission by their families to fly all the way over to Canada, anyway.'

'And Barber? He's an adult,' she pouted.

Marlene smiled and placed her hand on top of the teenager's.

'Barber is needed in London to help protect the students. As a Watcher yourself, surely you must understand that?'

Lana sighed, 'Yes of course I do. Sorry, I'm just worried.'

Declan smiled, 'We know.

But,' he lowered his voice to a whisper, 'your boyfriend is a pretty strong vampire. He can take care of himself,' he sniggered before adding, 'Everything is going to be fine, Lana.'

His wrinkled forehead, however, said something else entirely.

oOo

'HEY,' LANA SAID, WATCHING HER SISTER SLOWLY OPEN HER EYES as the plane finally came to a smooth halt on the tarmac.

'Hey, she yawned. 'Are we here?'

Lana nodded, 'Calgary airport.'

'What did Declan say?'

'The usual.'

'And your feeling about Scotland?'

Lana shrugged, 'We're in Alberta now. Not much we can do about it. Here,' she said, handing Emma her thick purple winter coat from the overhead locker.

'Thanks. It looks pretty cold out there.'

They both looked out of the window and saw a blanket of snow on either side of the runway, twinkling in the bright sunlight.

'Yeah, loads of snow,' Lana sighed, before adding. 'I feel so awful.'

'Don't you feel very well?' asked Emma.

'I feel fine. I just feel awful about this whole situation.'

'I don't follow you, Lana,' said Emma.

'We are the only ones that came to find her. It's not right. We should have the entire Watcher population out here searching for her.'

Emma groaned and plonked herself back on the seat while they waited for the other travellers to start leaving the aircraft.

'They have their reasons, we have to respect them.'

'We don't have to bloody like them though,' Lana said loudly, glancing backwards at Declan and the others, before delving into her handbag to find her lipstick.

Emma looked at her and pouted. 'You're right, we don't.'

'I just don't get it.'

'What?' asked Emma, getting a little exasperated.

'Why us? Why did they only choose the two of us to come with them? And why Aria and Marlene? Why not some of the others? Why couldn't Barber come? There's loads of other Watchers and Guardians to look after things in London and the rest of England for that matter? And why... why not your Diarmuid?'

'Diarmuid's mum said no. Simple as that.'

'It wasn't just his mum, Em, and you know it. They didn't let a lot of kids stop their studies to come and help.'

'It was mostly their parents though, really,' Emma replied. 'Their parents are worried as hell.'

'And ours weren't?' stated Lana. 'Mum and Dad didn't want us to come either but we made it quite clear there was no way in hell we weren't coming. The others could've done the same. They could have taken a stand, right?'

Emma lifted her eyebrows, 'It's not as simple as that, Sis. The other parents aren't as close to Declan like ours are. Declan saved Dad's life before, remember? They're like best mates. I reckon that's the main reason they let us come, because they know that Declan would lay down his life to save us. Plus, they know what Praxos means to us. They know what Eleanor means to us.'

'Maybe,' Lana sighed. 'Why us though?'

'Because Eleanor left strict instructions that if anything should happen, she wanted both of you to help us,' Declan said as he approached them from behind, making them both jump.

'Really?' Emma's eyes lit up.

Declan nodded, 'Girls, you must realise by now that you've both got something special going on. You're stronger than the majority of the Watchers that we know, adults included. Eleanor believes in you. She believes you will set us free.'

'Set us free?' Lana whispered. 'What does that mean?'

Declan shrugged ever so slightly, 'We're not entirely sure ourselves. Eleanor wrote it in a letter that Wilbur was keeping safe, only to be opened in the event of something happening to her.'

'What else did it say, Declan?' whispered Emma.

All the seats in front of them were now empty and a small queue was developing behind them.

'Oh sorry mate,' Declan said, moving out the way of a tall Chinese man who had cleared his throat, clearly trying to get their attention. He nodded respectfully as he passed.

'Look, I'll tell you more later. Let's just get off this plane first and sort ourselves out. Just...,' he pushed his hair back off his face, '...just... stop worrying. It's gonna be okay.'

Lana glanced at Emma and they both smiled, albeit with tight lips.

'Now c'mon, let's get out of here.'

$\maltese$ 2 $\maltese$

'Wow, it really is beautiful,' sighed Lana. 'I wish we were here under different circumstances, though,' she said, shivering as she zipped her coat right up to her chin.

'So this is Banff?' Emma said as she stepped out of the car and looked around at the warmly dressed people milling around. 'It's pretty.'

'Yes it is,' Aria smiled. 'It's a wonderful place for a holiday. Shame that's not why we're here though. This was one of the places John and I were planning to visit one day.' Her voice cracked and she cleared her throat. Looking away, she bit her lip before turning back to them. '

Come

on, let's head inside. Declan's already grabbed the bags,' she smiled as the girls followed her indoors.

'Well this is cozy,' Marlene said as she put the kettle on to make some tea and busied herself in the small open plan kitchen.

'So what happens now, Declan?' asked Lana. 'Is there a plan? Can you tell us more about the letter?'

'Come and sit down girls,' he ushered them onto the large old leather couch that faced the kitchen and then sat down on the armchair beside them.

'There's not an awful lot that you need to concern yourselves with right now girls. But if you must know, she left me instructions on running Praxos in London in the event of her dea..,' he stopped for a second, '... of something happening to her. But she did say that if something happened and she went missing, she was adamant that you both, the Morgan sisters, were to come and help find her. In the letter she told me how important you both are to Praxos - but I already knew that of course,' he looked up and smiled. 'And that she wanted you to work with us to find her.'

'But what about this whole setting us free business?' asked Lana.

Declan looked up at Aria and Marlene, 'We don't really understand what she means but she underlined it in her letter, so it's obviously something important.'.

Everyone was silent for a moment before Lana piped up, 'So what now? What's our next move?'

Declan stood up. Leaning against the fireplace, he sighed.

'What's the matter, Declan?' Emma asked, knowing something wasn't quite right.

'Well, here's the thing,' he eventually replied, turning to face them. 'We don't have any clues at the moment. All of our research seems to have come against a brick wall.'

Emma's eyes open wide, 'You mean all we're going on are our visions?'

Declan slowly nodded.

'But why?' Lana asked loudly.

'Let me guess,' Emma said somewhat bitterly. 'Because Eleanor told you to?'

'Pretty much. Look Emma, your vision with Eleanor was a strong one. You actually talked to her and she told you to come here. We're simply following that lead.'

'And then what?'

'Then we wait.'

'But waiting might be too late,' Emma yelled. 'She said they didn't have much time. She said to hurry.'

'Which is why we flew here immediately,' Marlene answered as she placed a few cups of tea on the coffee table in front of them.

'But what if that was wrong?' Lana said, exasperated. 'I told you it didn't feel right. I told you I think there's something going on with Scotland. What if she's there? What if John's there?'

Aria leaned against the inner archway that led to the bedrooms beyond, crossing her arms.

'We have to go on what Eleanor told Emma, Lana. It makes more sense. Why would Madge go to Scotland? Eleanor specifically said Canada and that's where we are now. We need you to work together to get down to detail. We need you to tell us what's next. We're counting on you.'

Emma burst into tears and ran out of the room.

'See?' Lana said. 'She just killed a man and now you're putting all this pressure on her to stop two more people from dying. Declan, this is...this is... this is crazy,' Lana seethed, standing up abruptly.

But when she got to where Aria stood, she stopped and let out a deep breath. Closing her eyes, she dropped her head backwards and took another deep breath before turning around.

'I'm sorry,' she whispered.

Declan smiled, his nostrils flaring slightly while he rubbed his chin, 'It's okay. I get it. I really do, mate and I'm sorry that this is all on you and your sister. It isn't fair but you are all we've got right now. Everyone and everything else has turned up nothing. I wish it was different, Lana, I really do but I believe in you both. Big time. I know you can do this,' he nodded. 'But you have to believe in yourselves too.'

'I'll go and speak to Emma,' she said, turning.

'No need. She heard me,' Declan smiled.

Emma gingerly appeared from the hallway wiping the tears from her eyes.

'I'm going to need some water.'

'I'll pour you a drink,' said Marlene, standing up.

Declan smiled and shook his head, 'She doesn't want a drink, Marlene. She wants to swim.'

oOo

'IT'S TOTALLY FROZEN OVER. ARE YOU SURE THIS IS A GOOD idea?' Marlene asked as they approached the nearby lake.

Lana and Declan smiled, 'Emma can thaw pretty much anything.'

'Oh right,' she said, looking a little confused.

'It would be quicker if Diarmuid was here to help me though,' Emma said as they found a spot that was totally isolated from the tourists that swamped the town.

'Is there anything we can do to help? Aria asked.

Emma shook her head, removing her clothes so she stood in just her swimsuit, before closing her eyes and concentrating hard on the task at hand.

'Do you want me to come in with you?' asked Lana who stood shivering next to Declan and the two women.

'Let me try alone first.'

Emma's body heat began to increase substantially until, eventually, she grinned as the ice below her gave way and she plunged into the icy lake.

The moment her body hit the water, Emma's heart soared. She was sure she was in the right place, she hoped so anyway.

'I hope she doesn't freeze down there,' Marlene said, a deep crease appearing down the middle of her forehead.

'You look so much like Eleanor when you do that,' Lana smiled. 'The old Eleanor.'

'Hey,' Marlene grinned, 'thanks very much.'

Chuckling, the group stepped backwards and waited patiently while Emma disappeared and swam deep beneath the frozen lake.

Although dark, Emma was amazed at the clarity of the water. She was able to light all around her using her unique ability to warm and lighten things up. Nestling on the bottom of the lake, she sat cross-legged and smiled to herself, waiting for inspiration to come.

Looking around, she was suddenly hit by a feeling of intense sadness and dread. It hit her in the stomach as if she'd been punched.

'Something's happened,' Declan said from the water's edge.

'Is she okay?' asked both Marlene and Aria at exactly the same time.

'She's fine,' Lana whispered. 'It's just a vision. I can feel it. Just... wait,' she breathed.

Beneath the surface, Emma was struggling to maintain calm within herself. The feeling had almost winded her, but she forced herself to take a couple of moments to understand what was happening. There didn't seem to be any actual visions, just feelings that were difficult to comprehend.

Closing her eyes again, Emma thought of nothing but Eleanor, yet her mind kept shifting to Madge and then to Sthenelaus. It was too much for her to take and she yelled at the top of her voice, letting water enter her lungs. She had to get out. Pushing herself from the bottom of the lake, Emma looked upward for the hole she'd made in the ice. Spotting it, she propelled herself out until she was laying on the ice, coughing.

Lana was first by her side, followed by Declan who gently picked her up and cradled her in his muscular arms.

'You're alright, shhhhh. Just breathe,' he said calmly. 'Take a few moments to let the breath come back to its natural state. Breathe. That's it.'

'She's shivering like crazy,' said Marlene as she and Aria wrapped blankets around her for comfort, as she was placed into the back of the car.

'Let's get her straight back to the house,' he said.

oOo

LANA SHOOK HER HEAD AS SHE WALKED BACK INTO THE LIVING room.

'Nothing at all?' Aria asked.

She shook her head again, 'All she said she got was a feeling of intense sadness and dread. She didn't see anything.'

'Poor thing,' Marlene said. 'Is she okay?'

Shrugging her shoulders, Lana sat down on the couch. 'She said she just needed half an hour on her own. But she's having a hot shower first.'

Everyone sat back. Nobody said a word.

In the shower, Emma curled up on the tiles and sobbed. She'd never felt such sadness before and it was overwhelming her, taking over her very being and she hated every second of it. She wanted to sleep, just sleep. So closing her eyes, she let the warmth of the water take her there.

'I just feel so awful that I haven't had any visions either,' Lana said quietly as she leaned forward on to her knees.

'Well, apart from the Scotland thing,' Aria added.

'Yeah but that wasn't really a vision, it was just a feeling.'

'And it still doesn't make any sense?' Declan asked.

Lana shook her head. 'No sense whatsoever and it's driving me crazy.'

The sound of a scream made all three of them jump up at once.

'Emma!' Lana screeched as she ran towards the bathroom, crashing through the door to find Emma lying naked on the floor of the shower, the water continuing to pour on top of her.

Lana quickly shut off the tap and grabbed the nearest towel, wrapping it carefully around her sister.

'Emma?' she whispered. 'Can you hear me?'

Aria and Marlene both stood by the door. 'What can we do?'

'We just need to get her out. Declan? It's ok, I've wrapped her in a towel.

He leaned over the shower and carefully lifted her up, carrying her into the girls bedroom where he placed her on the bed.

'She's still out,' he said. 'She must be having a vision.'

Lana nodded as Marlene appeared with a few more towels, placing some under her head while she gently mopped much of the water from her hair.

'Should we try and wake her?' she asked.

Lana shook her head, 'She needs to see it through to give us a better chance of finding them.'

Emma had the faintest sensation of being moved, but she didn't care. She was beneath the water again, but this time she wasn't alone. She'd been sitting silently there at the bottom of the lake when all of a sudden something was thrown into the water in front of her. It startled her so much that she screamed. Coming to her senses, she saw the object was large and heavy. Whatever it was appeared to be wrapped in something... a rug? Her eyes opened wide as she rushed to its side, unravelling the thick, heavy carpet until something rolled out of it.

It was the hair she noticed first. Long strands of blonde hair, moving gracefully through the water. She screamed, swimming away until she knew she had to go back. Slowly swimming towards it, she completely unravelled the carpet until she found the corpse of a beautiful woman. Her eyes were closed. More death. Sadness filled her every fibre once again as she tried to pull the body out of the water, but she was so heavy. Emma struggled until the corpse's eyes flew open, forcing Emma to scream out for the second time.

She wasn't dead? The woman's eyes turned a different colour and suddenly she was grappling to grab hold of something, anything. Her nails caught the side of Emma's face and she cried out in pain.

'Moraaiiinnnne,' the woman sang as she flailed about.

'Wait!'

Emma tried to yell but the muffled sounds of the water did little to help. 'I'm trying to help you. Let me help you. Stop fighting me and let me help you.'

But the woman's eyes suddenly changed back. The eyes of a corpse once again. It stopped moving and the body began to fall deeper and deeper beyond. Emma was helpless to do anything but watch until eventually, the body was swallowed by the darkened depths of the lake.

Emma's eyes opened suddenly and she coughed, struggling to sit up.

'Emma? It's okay, you're safe. You're safe,' Marlene reassured her as the tears began in earnest this time.

'Hey,' Lana said, sitting beside her and holding her hand.

Emma looked down and noticed she was wrapped in towels and her hair was still wet.

'What happened?'

'You had a vision in the shower and screamed. We thought we'd better get you out and somewhere warmer.'

Emma nodded before shaking her head, tears flowing faster now.

'Did you see something, Sis?'

'It was just a body in the lake. It didn't tell me anything about Eleanor,' she sniffed.

'It's okay,' Lana said, squeezing her hand. 'It might be a clue.

Don't disregard anything yet. You get dried up and into something warm and then we can talk about it, alright?'

Emma nodded, blowing her nose on the tissue that Marlene handed her.

'You're going to be alright, Emma,' she whispered as they all left her alone in the room to compose herself and get changed.

'I'm going to be alright,' she whispered to herself. 'I'm going to be alright.'

Ten minutes later, Emma entered the living room and smiled the best she could.

'Hey,' Declan said, standing up. 'Come on. Sit down and tell us what you saw.'

She nodded and repeated everything from the vision before continuing, '... and I think I need to swim again but not just anywhere. There's a specific lake I need to go to. There I'll understand what all this means.'

'Do you know which lake?' Aria asked.

'Moraine Lake,' she said matter-of-factly.

'How do you know?'

'She told me.'

Declan nodded. 'Okay then, we're headed to Moraine Lake. Do you want to rest first?'

But before he could finish the question, Emma was already putting on her coat and boots.

'Oh, okay. Let's go.'

❧   *3*   ❧

'I hear voices,' Declan whispered just after Emma had plunged into the water.

'Tourists?' asked Lana.

Declan strained a little bit before his eyes opened wide. He shook his head.

'No, not tourists. Oh no...'

'What is it Declan? You're scaring me?' Lana practically screeched.

But before he could answer, he had flung off his coat and dived into the freezing cold water.

'Declan no,' the three of them shouted after him.

'What the hell is he doing?' Lana cried. 'He won't survive that cold.'

'Yes he will,' Aria whispered calmly. 'Resurgam, remember?'

'Oh yeah, but... he has to die first to be able to come back,' she screeched again.

'He knows what he's doing, Lana. We have to support him,' Marlene said as she pulled Lana towards her and stopped her from doing anything silly. 'Just wait.'

Beneath the icy waters, Emma watched in disbelief as Declan swam, fully clothed, towards her.

'What are you doing?' she asked telepathically, knowing he could read her thoughts.

He pointed in the distance, shaking his head, mouthing 'danger'.

But Emma knew she had to stay, this was her only chance to find a clue as to Eleanor and John's whereabouts. She didn't know why it was here, she just knew she needed to be here. The dead woman had made that abundantly clear. Well, kind of. So she shook her head vehemently and turned to swim away. But before she did, she glanced back. That's when she noticed Declan wasn't looking so good. She grabbed him and held him tight, allowing her intense body heat to flow deep into his body.

At the same time, she finally saw what he had been warning her about.

They weren't alone.

There were three of them approaching, one woman and two men. Well, one female and two males. They certainly weren't human. Although Emma was pouring out intense heat all around her, she shivered. Declan, who was drifting in and out of consciousness, suddenly tensed up as he watched them approach.

'It's okay, Declan. They're not going to hurt us,' Emma thought, looking at him quickly before returning her gaze to the strange-looking creatures. Although their faces resembled humans, their bodies were scaly like that of large fish and when they opened their mouths, they were full of razor sharp teeth.

When they were about five metres away, they came to a stop and nodded towards them. The female of the group shifted slowly forward, her hands outstretched.

Declan immediately thrust himself between her and Emma, but Emma gently tugged him back.

'Declan, please go back. I'm safe. I can feel it. She needs to communicate with me.'

He was clearly unhappy about it, but after a few seconds, Declan nodded, using his last bit of strength to launch himself from the bottom of the lake, swimming as fast as he could until he reached his only exit from the cold water.

His friends rushed towards him, pulling him out and immediately warmed him with some of the towels they'd brought with them from their rental.

'What's happening Declan?' asked Lana as they rubbed him until colour began returning to his cheeks.

'She t...t...told me to...g....g....go.'

'Is she alright?'

He tried to nod.

Lana breathed heavily. 'Are you sure?'

'I think so,' he whispered. 'She's n....not alone though.'

'What?' yelled Lana. 'How could you leave her?'

Marlene put her hand on Lana's shoulder, 'Honey, he wouldn't have left her unless he thought she was safe. She'll be fine.'

'But...'

'No buts,' Marlene added. 'Have faith.'

'Faith?' Lana mouthed before turning away and shaking her head, stepping a few feet from them.

'Lana,' Declan shouted as she went to walk back towards the water. 'Don't do it. She's alright. I can hear her. Let her do her thing. Just take a breath and give her some space down there, okay?'

Lana bit her top lip and nodded before she took a long, deep breath and waited.

Beneath the water, Emma floated, carefully watching the creature as she gingerly moved closer. When her outstretched hands were close enough, Emma lifted both her arms until their hands touched - creating a gentle spark. The creature's terrifying mouth turned upwards into a smile and her entire face changed.

Emma watched in amazement as the woman standing before her was no longer the strange, frightening creature she'd seen moments before. It was Eleanor.

The water quickly disappeared and the two of them stood deep within a forest, surrounded by trees.

'Eleanor? What's happening? Where are you? We came to Canada but we can't find you anywhere.'

Eleanor nodded and smiled and motioned for Emma to follow her.

'Can't you just tell me where you are?'

Eleanor continued to smile, saying nothing as they walked, the ground crunching beneath their feet.

'Talk to me, Eleanor. I need to know.'

But she did nothing but smile.

'Jesus, Eleanor. What are we doing here?'

Eleanor stopped and turned to face her.

'Talk to me, please,' Emma pleaded, tears rolling down her face. 'I can't lose you, not now. Please just tell me, just tell me.'

Eleanor pointed to the trees around them.

'You're in a forest?'

Eleanor smiled.

'But where? Do these creatures have anything to do with this?'

Eleanor smiled.

'Are they responsible? Do they work for Madge?'

But Eleanor's face remained the same, making Emma become more and more irritated.

'If you're not going to tell me anything, then why did you bring me here? Why? I don't understand? You're not Eleanor. This is just a trick.'

Suddenly Eleanor grabbed Emma's hand and gently squeezed.

'What is it? What are you trying to tell me?'

Releasing her hand, the woman crouched down. Taking a stick, she used it to draw something in the dirt.

'You're trying to tell me something, aren't you?'

Eleanor slowly nodded.

Emma crouched down beside her. All she could see was one word.

'Magic? How does that help me?' she tutted, rubbing her forehead. 'I know about magic. We all have it. That doesn't help me, Eleanor. Help me help you,' she shouted. 'Magic what?'

Eleanor stood up and pointed to the trees again.

'I know, you're in a forest somewhere. In Canada? Which one? And what's magic?'

Eleanor just pointed at the trees.

'I don't understand, Eleanor. Magic trees? The magic is in the trees? I don't get it.'

The forest began to swirl and Emma felt like she was floating in water again. She opened her eyes, and the creatures were drifting off into the distance.

'Wait!' she tried to shout but seconds later, they were gone and Emma had no choice but to return to the surface.

'Emma!' Lana yelled, running as fast as she could towards her sister who had jumped so far out of the water that she was further away than before. 'Are you alright? I was so worried.'

'I'm okay, Sis. I'm fine,' Emma said, as she used her own skills to warm herself up. 'Let's just get back to the house.'

oOo

'MAGIC TREES? THAT'S WHAT SHE TOLD YOU?'

Emma sighed for the fourth time, 'Yes, Jesus, how many times do I have to tell you? That's all she managed to tell me. And what the hell was that creature anyway? And why did she help us? I'm so confused, I don't understand any of this.'

'You're not the only one, Emma. We're all confused. This is messed up,' Declan said, as he put on another thick jumper on top of the one he was already wearing.

'Still cold, huh?' Marlene asked. 'Maybe you should take a hot bath?'

'I will, in a bit,' he smiled. 'After we've figured this out.'

Marlene nodded while they made themselves comfortable in the same place they'd sat earlier in the day, surrounding the fire.

'Do you know what they were, Declan?' Lana asked.

'Those creatures?'

She nodded.

'Honestly, I've no idea. Initially I thought maybe mermaids, but living in a lake? I dunno.'

'Maybe they don't live there. Maybe they were just travellers. Maybe Eleanor somehow managed to communicate with them while they were passing through,' Aria thought out loud.

'Passing through where exactly?' Emma asked.

Nobody answered.

'I just feel like we're getting further and further from the truth. Why can't she just tell us?'

'Do you think it was really her?' Lana asked. 'How do we know it's not some kind of trick? Madge could have put them up to it.'

'No, it was her,' Emma said.

'But how do you know?' Lana asked.

'I just do.'

'Fair enough,' Lana answered back as she tossed another log onto the fire.

As they watched the flames dance around and envelope the wood, Emma suddenly perked up, her eyes wide. 'Magic trees!' she exclaimed. 'She was telling me she needs somebody else's help. Oh why didn't I see that to begin with?'

'Who, Sis, who?' asked Lana.

Declan nodded, 'You're right. You're absolutely right. I'll get on the blower straight away.'

'On the blower?' asked Aria as Lana stood up with her hands on her hips.

'Who?' Lana asked for the second time.

'Oh, that just means he's going to make a phone call, Aria,' smiled Marlene.

'Strange English language,' muttered Aria as Lana became more exasperated.

'Who are you calling?' Lana demanded for the third time.

'Why Sammy, of course,' Emma smiled.

❧ 4 ☙

She was one of the ugliest women ever to have been born, but Madge Sophokles had accepted it pretty early on in life and had therefore never really let it bother her. She'd married a very wealthy man - also a Skull - who was equally hideous, both in looks and personality, but she had soon grown bored of his uselessness. Her attempts at poisoning him had not quite come to fruition so she had simply let him be caught by the Watchers and had been overjoyed to hear that he'd eventually been killed in captivity.

Sthenelaus did have some use, however, having aided her into becoming one of the most powerful Skulls in England. But that wasn't enough for her. She wanted more. Madge wanted to be the most powerful Skull in the world. And to do that, she would have to do away with the Watchers once and for all.

Madge believed that kidnapping Eleanor Hayden-Jones, the Guardian of the Fourth House of Praxos, was a stroke of genius. It was her way of getting exactly what she wanted. It was her way in.

'Has she arrived yet?' asked Madge, placing the hand mirror back down onto the desk and turning in her swivel seat to look out at the forest.

'No Ma'am, not yet,' said the nervous young man who looked oddly out of place wearing clothing that resembled an outfit from several centuries ago.

'Valentine, get out there and don't come back in until she's arrived.'

'Yes Ma'am,' he nodded, backing out of the room and closing the door behind him.

'I still can't quite believe that this spell is going to work,' said a man's voice in the corner.

'I can. I can do anything I want to do and I'm disgusted you don't believe that,' she scowled, standing up and staring at him.

'I'm, I'm sorry, I didn't mean that I didn't believe in you, Madge. That's not what I meant at all. I just meant...'

'I don't care what you meant, you little...'

She was interrupted by a quiet knock on the door.

'Yes?' she bellowed, walking around the front of the large walnut desk. Leaning against it, she momentarily glanced out of the room's other window, looking down towards the ocean beyond.

The door was gingerly pushed open and the same oddly dressed young man poked his head around it. 'She's here, Ma'am. She's arrived.'

Madge nodded before the door was pushed all the way open to allow an elderly woman to stride in.

'Well, it's about time. I've been waiting for days,' Madge stated.

'Yes well, my apologies, but this isn't the easiest of locations to find and these things take time, Mrs. Sophokles.

'Oh don't call me that, for heaven's sake. My name is Madge and I'm proud of it.'

Nodding, the elderly woman took off a long cloak and a headscarf.

'Very well, Madge it is. Now, if you don't mind, I require a drink.'

'Of course,' said Madge.

'Valentine, get in here,' Madge shouted.

The oddly dressed young man appeared, 'Ma'am?'

'A drink for the old lady.'

'Less of the old,' she murmured before turning to face Valentine. 'Whisky. And make it a large one,' she smiled.

Valentine nodded. 'And for you, Ma'am?'

'Yes, my usual.'

Valentine backed out of the room, returning just moments later with a tray containing two large glasses, one full of an amber coloured liquid while the other was clear.

'Vodka? Gin?' asked the old lady as she took a long sip of her warming whisky.

'Holy water.'

The woman croaked with laughter. 'Nice touch.'

'It is, isn't it? Madge smiled. 'Now, let's get down to business.'

'Of course. It is why I'm here,' the elderly lady said as she opened the old leather bag she'd carried in with her.

Taking out a small glass bottle, she placed it on the desk in front of her.

'This should do the trick.'

'Is it what I asked for?'

'Don't I always get what you ask for?'

'There has been the odd occasion when you've failed me, Geraldine.'

Geraldine scowled, 'That was in the early days. Things have changed since then.

'Don't I know it,' Madge grinned, her ugliness making Geraldine squirm a little. 'How long will it take?'

'Should be instant.'

'Very well. How long will it last?'

'Weeks, I think.'

Madge's face grew thunderous and she banged her fists on the desk, 'You think?'

'It's an intricate spell Madge, and it required certain things that were not easy to come by. I was forced to use a little less than I would have liked.

'Here you are, failing me again, Geraldine,' Madge shouted.

'I have not failed you. I have provided you with the potion you asked for. Not once did you tell me it was meant to be permanent or at least semi-permanent. I have produced what I could with the ingredients I could get at this short notice. Take it or leave it.'

Madge scowled before a smile crept onto her face. 'Very well.'

'My payment?' Geraldine asked.

'As agreed,' Madge replied before she stood up and approached the man in the corner.

'This is him, as promised.'

Geraldine grinned from ear to ear. 'A fine specimen, Madge. He will do nicely.'

'What?' said the man as he stood from his corner seat. 'What are you doing? I have been good to you, Madge. I have always done what you asked of me. Why would you do this? What will happen to me? What will she do to me?'

Suddenly his free hands were no longer free and he found himself unable to speak.

Geraldine was standing, her arms high above her head as she muttered something in a strange language. The man's eyes grew weary and moments later, he collapsed onto the floor.

'Wonderful!' Madge clapped. 'I do enjoy watching you work your magic, Geraldine. Out of curiosity, what will you do with him?'

Geraldine smiled as she knocked back the remaining whisky before wrapping the cloak around herself, and placing the head scarf back over her head.

'You told me he had vampire blood in his veins?'

Madge nodded, 'For certain.'

'Then I will simply drain him.'

'And his blood?'

Geraldine smiled, 'I cannot say. I am sworn to secrecy by my coven.'

'Very well, whatever,' Madge scowled. 'It was our deal, you do with him whatever you wish. That's your business. This,' she said picking up the bottle, 'is mine.'

'Why now, Madge? After all these years?'

'I have my reasons, Geraldine. You will find out soon enough. I know how word gets around in our circles,' she smirked.

Geraldine smiled. 'Yes, yes, it does. Well, enjoy it while you can.'

❦ *5* ❦

Yawning loudly and rushing through the airport, Sammy smiled at the approaching group while she dragged her hand luggage behind her.

'Sammy!' shrieked Lana, almost knocking her to the ground with a spine-crushing hug.

'Hey guys,' she just about managed to breathe. 'How's it going? Found anything yet? I'm so glad you called me over. I felt so useless at home. Everyone does, actually.'

'Hey Sammy,' Emma said, giving her a quick hug before shoving her hands in her jacket pockets before shaking her head. 'Practically nothing, which is why you're here.'

'Yeah, about that. Declan was pretty cryptic over the phone. What's going on? Why do you need me? I mean, I'm flattered but confused.'

'We'll update you in the car. Declan and the others are waiting outside.'

oOo

'So you think it's got something to do with the trees, then?' Sammy asked as they drove down the wide Canadian highway back towards Banff after they'd explained everything to her.

Everyone nodded.

'Which is why you need me?'

Again, more nodding.

'But which trees? I can't just talk to any old tree, you know? I mean, yeah I can - obviously. But not all trees are going to know what's going on. It's not like every tree is like the Tree of Tonuka, you know.'

'Yeah we know that, Sammy, and we haven't figured it out yet. We're just hoping you can work your magic with Emma and Lana,' Declan said from the driver's seat.

Sammy sat back and nodded. 'Well, I'll do everything physically possible to get Eleanor back.'

'And John,' Aria murmured, looking out of the window so the others couldn't see her damp eyes.

'Yes, yeah of course,' Sammy replied, blushing ever so slightly. 'Oh, Gosh I almost forgot to tell you.'

'What?' asked Lana.

'The gang at home, they're getting so restless. They really wanna help. Diarmuid is tearing his hair out, poor thing - oh by the way, Emma, he told me to tell you that he really misses you and hates that he couldn't come too, but I guess you already knew that. He's constantly sending you messages, isn't he?'

Emma just smiled.

'But seriously, Declan. Everyone is on standby to help. Anything. They know they can't come over but anything they can do at home, just say the word. We were all feeling pretty useless.'

'Thanks Sammy, I know. Did you ask them to look into the creatures at the lake?'

Sammy nodded, 'Yeah, Daisy and Beau decided to look into that. Beau said he'd let us know the second they find anything useful.'

'Cool, thanks,' Declan, said as he glanced at her via the rearview mirror.

'Oh, another thing,' she suddenly remembered. 'Moira told me to tell you she keeps dreaming the same three words and she doesn't understand why.'

'Oh yeah, what words?'

'Erm, oh, I can't remember. Here, I wrote them down,' she shuffled around in her jacket until she pulled out a crumpled piece of paper. Unravelling it, she slowly read, 'Tempus Edax Rerum.'

'Time, devourer of all things,' Declan whispered.

'Huh? Declan?'

'What's that really mean though, Declan?' asked Lana from the very back of the vehicle.

He shook his head, 'I'm not sure.'

'It means that we're running out of time,' Emma said quietly.

Everyone grew silent. Instead, they just watched the snow covered mountains in the distance, each one thinking about the task ahead, hoping that the captives would soon be found safe. Suddenly, Emma sat bolt upright, 'Oh My God,' she shrieked, making Declan slam on the brakes.

'What?! What is it Em?'

'Tempus Edax Rerum.'

'What? What about it?' asked Lana.

'It doesn't just mean time devourer of all things.'

'No? Well what else does it mean.'

'It's Imran. Those were Imran's words.'

'What do you mean, Emma?' asked Aria from the front passenger seat.

'Imran was our friend, a Watcher. He died last year.'

Declan sighed, and began driving again.

'Don't you see, Declan? It must be connected.'

'Or Moira might just be dreaming about an old friend.'

'No, Moira never has meaningless dreams. They always relate to what's going on at the Academy.'

He raised his eyebrows, 'Yeah, I suppose you're right. But when Imran was trying to contact us before, didn't he do it through Nisha?'

'Yes, but maybe this time, he can't, because Nisha is in Pakistan, right?'

Declan nodded. 'Well, it's something to consider, I suppose.'

'Hey,' suddenly Aria piped up, pointing out the window. 'I've seen that before.'

Declan slowed down the van again and pulled over to the side of the road.

'What?'

'You see that mountain over there?'

'Erm, we're kind of surrounded by mountains here,' Lana replied, clearly unimpressed.

'No, that one, right there. Sthenelaus had a picture of it on his office wall.'

Lana pulled a face, 'It's the Rockies, don't lots of people have landscapes like those on their walls?'

'No, this is different. That picture meant something to him.'

'Is there a way up there?' asked Marlene.

'There,' Aria pointed to a sign in the distance. I think there might be a road. We should check it out.'

'And this is exactly why we brought Aria with us, girls,' Declan grinned. 'Looks like we might be on to something.'

'Like a wild goose chase,' Lana murmured quietly before Emma gently elbowed her sister in the ribs.

When they followed Aria's clue, the road lead them to a further smaller track covered in snow, which, in turn, led them to a large, log cabin.

'This is it, guys,' Aria yelled, as she jumped out of the van first and ran up to the main entrance, almost slipping on the ice.

'Wait, Aria. It could be dangerous,' Marlene yelled after her.

'No, there's nobody here,' Declan said, listening for voices in his head before following them. 'I'm pretty sure it's empty.'

Soon they had exited the van and were all standing by the door while Declan peered into the window.

'Well, are we going to go in?' Lana asked as she rubbed her gloved hands together. 'It's freezing out here.'

'It definitely looks empty, so yes, let's get inside,' Aria replied.

As Aria placed her fingers on the large handle, the door practically swung open, almost inviting them in from the cold.

'Be careful,' said Declan. 'Could be a trap.'

They gingerly stepped inside, finding nothing but a near-empty property.

'Doesn't look like anyone was here recently,' Emma sighed as she stood in the centre of the main room, looking around. 'There's nothing here.'

'Exactly, I knew we weren't going to find anything here. It's just a waste of ti...' but before she could finish her sentence, Lana had collapsed on the floor.

'Sis!' shouted Emma. 'Guys, help!'

They rushed forward, Declan picking up the seventeen-year-old Watcher before finding an old wooden table to place her on.

'Is she alright?' whispered Marlene as they all peered down at her.

Emma held tightly on to Lana's hand and nodded. 'I think she's having a vision of some kind.'

oOo

'STHENELAUS? BUT YOU'RE DEAD. EMMA KILLED YOU,' WHISPERED Lana as she stood watching the most evil man she'd ever laid eyes on. He was standing, looking out of the window in the cabin. But there was no snow outside and the sun was shining.

'What are you up to?' she whispered to herself.

As he turned, she noticed he was talking to someone. She looked around and found herself face to face with the ugliest woman she'd ever seen. Madge.

'Well?' asked Madge. 'Is it done?'

Sthenelaus nodded, his cruel face twisting into what appeared to be a smile.

'Of course, my dear. You asked and I have arranged it. The house is ours.'

Madge nodded, 'Excellent. I will arrange the rest. You can leave that to me.'

'When do we move in?' he asked.

Lana watched as, unbeknown to her husband, Madge cringed before attempting a smile. The woman turned back towards him, 'In a few months, after I've organised a few things first. You haven't mentioned this to Aria have you?'

'No, you said you wanted a house that was all your own, one that didn't include my second wife. I have done as you asked.'

'So you will not mention my new abode to her at all?'

'Not if you don't want me to. But why the secrecy? She is also my wife, Madge. We're supposed to be living all of us together.'

'Which we do... in England. But here, I'd rather have my own space; a little independence of my own.'

'Very well then, my dear. My lips are sealed. But why there? Why not here? Alberta is far more beautiful?'

'Yes, Alberta certainly has its appeal and this cabin is acceptable, I suppose, but it's yours. I want my own home, over there.'

'Where?!' Lana screamed with frustration. 'Just say it,' she said, tiptoeing around the woman. 'Tell me where you are, you witch. Where are you? Where are you keeping Eleanor?'

'Besides, it's a much shorter journey. You know how I hate to travel.'

'Yes, yes, my dear. Anything you want,' Sthenelaus muttered. 'Anything at all, it's yours.'

'Yes I know, Sthen. I can have everything I want and I will... in time.'

Lana watched as the woman's grin grew larger as she walked out of the room.

'Where is it, Sthenelaus? Where is this house?' Lana asked, knowing full well he couldn't see, or hear her.

Once Madge had gone, her husband returned his attention to the window, before picking up his phone and dialling a number.

'Book me a flight home...tomorrow. I have business to attend to. Oh and book one for Madge too, but not for home. She's going to the new place to decorate. Book her a flight to...'

Before the word escaped his lips, Lana felt herself grow faint.

'No, not now. I'm so damn close. Wait, wait.'

But it was useless. Her vision had come to an abrupt end. She slumped to the floor.

oOo

THE SMELL OF WOOD FILLED HER NOSTRILS. SOMEONE WAS gripping tightly to her hand. Turning her head, she opened her eyes. 'Em?'

'I'm here, Lana. I'm right here.'

Declan and Emma helped her sit upright as she took in a deep breath through her open mouth.

'What happened?' asked Aria, 'Did you discover anything new?'

Lana sighed. 'Kind of, but the vision cut me off just before I could find out the most crucial bit.

Sthenelaus bought Madge a house of her own somewhere. I reckon that must be where they are.'

'But where?' asked Emma.

'That's the tricky bit, she never actually said it.'

'Jesus,' Emma said through gritted teeth. 'This is just getting worse by the minute.'

'I'm sorry, Sis,' Lana whispered.

'It's not your fault,' Emma shook her head and frowned. 'Just tell us everything that was said. Maybe we can work it out.'

'I've searched the rest of the house and there's nothing here. She must've cleared it out after Sthenelaus died,' Marlene said, walking back into the main room. 'I don't think we'll find anything else here. Let's head back to our place.'

Declan nodded as he helped Lana down off the table.

'Tell us the rest in the car. Come on, let's get out of here. This place gives me the creeps,' he said.

'You and me both,' Emma whispered as they shut the door behind them and returned to their hired van.

❦   6   ❧

A large map of Canada was spread out over the dining table as the group stood, all holding hot cups of tea and coffee, poring over it.

'It's a shorter journey, that's the main thing,' Lana said.

'Are you sure it's in Canada though?' asked Marlene as she walked the length of the table.

'Definitely,' Lana said, leaning over to see if anything would jump out at her.

'OMG. I don't believe it,' she suddenly cried.

'What?' Emma asked.

'It's been right under my nose this whole time and nobody figured it out. God, we're so stupid. We need to go. Now.'

Declan immediately nodded, looking a little ashamed. 'I'm sorry, Lana. Sometimes we just don't see things that are really obvious. I should have trusted you and your feelings.'

'What? What the heck are you talking about? Will you please tell us,' Emma sighed.

'Nova Scotia.'

'Nova Scotia? But why would you know that? Why was it under your nose? I don't get it.'

'Scotland, Emma. All this time I kept getting that feeling we should been going to Scotland. Nova Scotia means New Scotland.'

'Oh no,' Emma cried.

. . .

oOo

A few hours later, the group had managed to secure a flight to Halifax, the capital of Nova Scotia and were all eager to get there, knowing they were finally getting closer to Eleanor and John.

'Do you know where we're headed yet?' asked Emma.

Lana shook her head, 'Declan wants to wait until we arrive before booking anything, just in case either of us manages to see anything else in the meantime.'

Emma nodded.

'Maybe we should try and get some sleep? It might help. And you never know, visions could come then.'

'Yeah, you're right,' she replied, trying to get comfortable before she closed her eyes.

Sammy was busy listening to music with her headphones while sketching trees on a pad of paper, so Lana sat quietly watching her sister drift off to sleep before she silently climbed out of her seat and walked to the back of the plane to where Declan, Aria and Marlene sat.

'You alright, mate?' Declan asked.

Lana nodded as she stretched her legs. 'Yeah, just wondering what the plan is when we get there?'

'Well, we were just talking about that. We reckon we're looking for somewhere quiet, somewhere off the beaten track, perhaps. But more importantly, it's got to be somewhere surrounded by trees. A forest or something.'

Nodding, Lana leaned sideways on his seat to look at the smaller map he was holding up.

'There,' she pointed. 'Cape Breton Highlands Park. It's miles from anywhere and huge. I reckon that's where she is.'

Declan looked up and smiled, 'I was thinking the exact same thing. But it's a big place. We're gonna have our work cut out for us.'

'Yeah,' smiled Lana. 'But this time we've got a secret weapon.'

Both of them turned to look towards Sammy.

'Not many people can communicate with trees.'

'And animals, for that matter,' Declan added. 'In the park, that might just be what we need.'

oOo

Emma stood next to a hospital bed. Beside her was a dead body covered from head to toe with a white sheet. But she didn't need to remove it to see who it was. Sthenelaus.

She'd done that to him. She'd killed him. He'd forced her into it, of course. But she'd still done it.

She'd killed a man.

Suddenly, an intense pain in her lower back overcame her and she was forced down onto her knees in agony.

'Noooooo,' she yelled as she grappled to pull up her jumper to see what was happening. Turning, she found herself looking into a full length mirror.

She twisted her body and lifted her top further. Her tattoo had changed.

No longer was there an eye with majestic wings. In its place was a skull with broken wings beside it.

Emma's eyes opened wide and she tried to scream but no sound would come out of her mouth. She stood staring at herself, terrified, when Sthenelaus suddenly appeared behind her, laughing, taunting her. 'You're one of us now,' he whispered into her ear.

'Aaaaaargh,' she screamed.

Immediately, Lana was by her side trying to calm her down.

'Hey, hey. It's okay, it's okay, Sis. You're safe. We're on a plane and you're completely safe. What did you see? Was it a vision?'

Emma shook her head and swallowed.

'Just a bad dream?' asked Sammy, who had removed her headphones and was reaching for a bottle of water from her bag by her feet.

Emma nodded, 'Just a bad dream, just a bad dream,' she repeated over and over again.

'Here, have a sip of water. It'll do you good,' Sammy handed her the bottle, removing the cap.

'Shhhhh, Sis. It was nothing but a dream.'

'Just a bad dream, just a bad dream, just a bad dream,' Emma continued, rocking her head back and forth.

Sammy glanced at Lana with concern, before eyeing Declan who had rushed down the aisle.

'Hey, what's going on?'

But before anyone could say anything, he motioned for Lana to get out of her seat. He sat down in her place and gently pulled Emma into his arms, shushing and rocking her like a child.

'It was a bad one, huh?' he asked.

Emma didn't reply.

'Just a bad dream?' Declan said. 'You're right, it was just a bad dream. Now take a breath, slowly in and out. Listen to my voice and let it soothe you, gently does it. Breathe in, breathe out, that's it, mate. Shhhhh. You're going to be fine.'

Sammy and Lana just watched, giving each other a strange look, wondering what she'd dreamed about that was so bad. Although Lana did have an idea.

'Shhhhhh, mate. Just a bad one, that's all. You're fine. Close your eyes and just listen to my voice. Easy does it.'

Declan looked up to Lana for a second and nodded, motioning for her to take his seat at the back.

'I'll stay with her. She'll be alright,' he whispered, before returning his attention to Emma who was slowly going back to sleep.

Sammy watched Lana walk away before she put her headphones back on and continued drawing.

'What happened?' asked Marlene and Aria once Lana was sitting beside them.

'Em had a really bad dream.'

'What about?' Aria asked.

'She didn't say but I reckon it was about killing Sthenelaus again.'

Marlene patted Lana on the hand and smiled sadly. 'It's takes time to get over something like that.'

'Have you?'

Marlene lifted her brows.

'Killed anyone?' Lana whispered.

Marlene looked around for a second before slowly nodding,

'Sometimes, it has been inevitable. But in every case, death was the only way.'

Lana nodded.

'It hardens you in a way you cannot imagine, but you can learn to live with it, especially as Watchers. But the dreams are always the worst. They will pass though. Emma will be okay. She's stronger than you think, you know?'

'What do you mean? I know she's strong?'

'But you worry more about her than about you? I can see that.'

'She's my sister, of course I do.'

'Yes I understand that, but you do not give her the credit she deserves.'

'I do,' Lana replied defensively.

'Not in the way she needs it. At the moment you are a team, you two. But it will not always be so.'

Lana's expression changed and she looked up, distraught.

'It is something you must accept, Lana. You cannot always be together. You have two paths to go down. They cannot be the same.'

Lana looked puzzled.

Marlene smiled.

'You will always be sisters and you will always be Watchers but you have different destinies. You are two people, not one. You must trust that she is strong, she can protect herself.'

'How do you know all this?'

'I am a Watcher, and I am Eleanor's daughter. I've been around for a long time and I do have certain skills of my own,' she said, smiling. 'But I can also see the obvious. You are very different from each other. Emma will take a different path from you. You are more like me, Lana. You are a fighter, whereas Emma is a natural carer. I believe she will be a healer. Actually, I have a feeling she will be one of the best healers the Watchers have ever seen.'

'Really?' Lana said. 'You can see that for her?'

'Naturally. I think you have seen it for yourself, have you not?'

Lana smiled and nodded, looking down the aisle to where her sister was sitting with Declan.

'What about me?' she asked. 'What do you see?'

'I see a headstrong, passionate young woman with a fondness

for adrenaline,' Marlene grinned. 'You will be... no, I will not tell what you will be. That, you must work out for yourself.'

'Oh, Marlene, please tell me. I want to know.'

But Marlene shook her head, 'Lana, I think deep down you already do.'

Lana gulped loudly and smiled. 'Maybe.'

❧ 7 ❧

The Cape Breton Highlands were quite a distance from Halifax, so Declan, Aria and Marlene took it in turns to do the driving; with Lana complaining several times that she ought to be allowed to drive every once in a while.

She'd given some thought to what Marlene had said on the plane and realised she was absolutely right. She did love adrenaline and there were so may things she wanted to try, driving being one of them.

'But now is not the right time to learn,' Declan had scolded her.

'But I think I already know, Declan,' she said, sticking out her tongue like a child as he climbed back into the driver's seat.

'How can you already know?' he asked. 'You've never even had any lessons.'

'I know, weird right?' she grinned.

He shook his head and laughed at her. 'Something tells me you're going to prove me wrong, but not on this trip, okay?'

Lana gave in and sat back, closing her eyes like the other girls had.

Emma meanwhile, hadn't said much since her bad dream. The first thing she had done though, was to find a mirror so she could reassure herself that her tattoo remained the same.

She'd breathed a huge sigh of relief to find it unchanged; a beautiful winged eye with words beneath it,

Lux in Tenebris Lucet.

Feeling a little more content within herself, she'd followed the rest of the group through the airport, waited at the hire car desk and then had hopped into the van with the rest of them. Somehow, something had changed within her. She was feeling closer to Eleanor and that made her more feel slightly more satisfied.

'Does anyone else feel more positive?' asked Lana.

'What do you mean?' Sammy replied.

'I don't know, really. I just feel like we're finally on the right tracks.'

'I do too,' Emma said quietly. 'I feel like she's closer to us.'

'Eleanor?' asked Sammy.

Emma nodded, 'Yes, she's here somewhere.'

'What about my John?' Aria whispered. 'Do you feel him?'

Emma looked sad, 'I don't really have a connection to him, so I can't say. Sorry Aria.'

Aria looked down, 'That's okay, it was silly to think you would have.'

'Hey,' Sammy pointed. 'Look!'

'What?' asked Lana.

'Trees!' she yelped, as they spotted the first trees at the opening to a huge forest, dusted with snow.

Declan laughed as he brought the vehicle to a standstill.

'You ready to try and have a chat?' he asked.

Sammy, glowing, nodded avidly. 'Yes, let's get this party started!'

Lana chuckled as they all clambered out of the vehicle and walked up to the nearest tree.

'No, not the nearest one. I need to talk to one which is surrounded by others. See what I can get from that beauty over there,' she pointed.

The others followed her as she wandered through the first batch of trees, into a darker area of the forest, stumbling over a huge mass of twisted roots.

'Isn't it beautiful?' she asked as she found the oldest tree to touch.

The moment her fingers traced the bark, her body relaxed and she melted into it, like she was giving it a huge hug.

The others found somewhere to sit or lean against, dusting the snow away. They just waited patiently, hoping Sammy would be able to communicate with this incredible gentle giant of a tree.

As Sammy did her bit, Lana sat beside Emma and squeezed her hand. 'You feeling okay, Sis?' she asked, drawing a long strand of black hair away from her sister's emerald green eyes.

'Yeah, I think so.'

'That dream really got to you, huh?'

Emma nodded.

'But you're gonna be okay, yeah?'

'Sure,' Emma smiled. 'When I was sitting with Declan on the plane, I was overcome with this feeling of peace, but it was only after I'd checked my tattoo that I realised I'll be alright.'

'Your tattoo?'

'Yeah, it was horrible, Lana. I dreamt it changed to a Skull tattoo. Sthenelaus told me I'd become one of them.'

'Ouch, that's a horrible dream.'

'I know, right?'

Lana nodded, 'But you do know that could never happen, right?'

'Yeah I guess so.'

'Well, I know so. I have it on good authority.'

Emma looked quizzically at her sister, who, in turn, looked towards Marlene who sat some distance away with her eyes closed. But she was smiling, as if she could hear them.

'Marlene? What did she tell you?'

'Just that you're gonna be great,' Lana laughed, making Emma look even more confused.

'Great? Me? Really? At what, exactly?'

'At everything you do, hon.'

'Oh...okay then.'

Sammy was humming gently, a sound that soon seemed to echo all around them. It was so beautiful, an ethereal sound that appeared to emanate throughout the forest, from beneath the ground to the tops of the trees. Sammy was smiling now and nodding occasionally, stroking her hands against the old trunk of the tree. She lifted her face and opened her eyes, watching the bare branches gently sway in the breeze, before she loosened her grip and turned to the others.

Her smile dropped a little before she shook her head.

'Nothing?' asked Declan.

'Not much, I'm afraid. I think we might still be too far away.'

'But what did you find out?'

'There have been lots of people around here lately. Lots of walkers, photographers, hikers. This tree could not pinpoint anything really evil. She spoke with her sisters surrounding us but nothing to really recall. Nothing that could really help us. She suggested we continue north though.'

'North it is then,' Declan said as he helped Sammy climb back over some of the higher roots jutting out of the ground. 'Thanks for trying Sammy.'

'Oh, that's alright. There'll be other trees to talk to. The right ones are coming.'

Declan squinted in the sunlight and nodded. 'I'm sure they are.'

As Emma and Lana stood up and began walking back to the van, Emma stumbled. Lana leaned forward to catch her but ended up falling along with her. As they fell to the ground, time seemed to slow down, as if they were falling in slow motion.

Once both were on their hands and knees, Lana looked at her sister.

'You alright, Sis?'

'Yeah, but where are we...'

'Huh?' asked Lana.

'What's going on?' asked Emma as Lana suddenly realised they were no longer amidst the same trees with the rest of the gang. 'Where are we?'

'Must be another vision,' Emma whispered as she stood, dusting the powdery snow from her jeans.

'It's a strong one if we're both having it,' Lana agreed.

'Where do you think we are?' Emma asked as they looked around.

Tall trees surrounded them, much like before, and snow covered some areas of the ground beneath their feet.

'I don't know. Wait, look,' she pointed off into the distance.

'Is that water?'

Emma nodded. 'It's the ocean.'

'So we've somehow come to the coast?'

'I guess so,' Emma answered as they held on to each other before they began gingerly walking through the forest to get a better look at their surroundings.

'What do you reckon?' asked Lana as they looked down the towards the rocky outcrop to the water below. 'It looks freezing,' she shivered.

Emma smiled, 'Probably but not a problem.'

'Huh? Surely you don't want to go for a swim now? You can't anyway. Not in a vision. Can you?'

'I don't see why not, but there's no need. There's nothing pulling me down there.'

'Which way is it pulling you?' Lana asked, looking behind them at the hillside covered in trees.

'I honestly don't know. What about you?'

'I'm not sure,' Lana whispered, putting her gloved hands into the pockets of her thick parka.

'Why the vision then?' Emma asked. 'Our visions are normally telling us something. What's this supposed to be telling us?'

'Maybe she's near here somewhere?' Lana replied.

'I wish she could just appear and tell us.'

'Hey, did you hear that?' Lana suddenly asked, turning towards her sister.

'No, what?'

'Listen,' Lana said.

Both girls stood silently for a moment.

'I don't hear anything,' Emma said impatiently.

'Shhhhhh.' Lana commanded.

'Music, it sounds like a...like a harp,' Emma whispered.

'Yeah, but why on earth can we hear a harp out here in the middle of nowhere?'

'Is it coming from...up there?' Emma whispered again as they both looked up towards the sky.

'No, no way,' Lana replied. 'That's just freaky.'

'And our lives in general aren't freaky?' Emma asked as they both stood craning their necks upwards to try and hear it more clearly.

'It's definitely a harp, and it's definitely coming from up there,' Lana pointed to the sky again. 'But what does it mean?'

'I haven't got a clue.'

'Do you think it's the...the... angels?' Lana asked, feeling a little stupid for asking the question in the first place.

But Emma nodded, 'I think it might well be.'

'It could actually be our...our...m...'

'Birth mother?' asked Emma, with her eyebrows lifted.

Lana shrugged her shoulders, 'A stupid thought, I know. I just don't understand any of what's going on at the moment. It's like everything is changing. None of our usual methods seem to be working the way they normally do. Since Eleanor was taken, I just,' she sighed. 'I'm just so confused, Sis. I wish I knew the answers. I just want everything to be back to normal again, you know?'

Emma nodded and stepped backwards, looking for a large smooth rock or tree stump to sit on, 'Let's just sit down for a bit and...'

'And what? Wait? Listen?' Lana threw her arms up in the air before her shoulders slumped forward and she nodded in agreement. 'Okay.'

After a couple of minutes of sitting quietly, listening to the soothing sounds of what appeared to be a harp being played in the sky, Emma suddenly perked up.

'What? You see something?' Lana asked.

'No, but that song. I've heard it before.'

'You have?'

'Listen,' Emma encouraged Lana to sit quietly again and just listen.

After another minute, the sounds ceased.

'Figure it out?' Lana asked in a whisper.

Emma nodded, 'Well I think so, at least the music anyway.'

'Tell me?'

'It's a really old song. I mean really old. Mum listens to it sometimes. She's got some album with it on. I think it's that woman with the really short hair. You know, the old woman?'

'Yeah, Sis, that really helps. I need something else to go on.'

'I think she might be known for her charity work. For AIDS or something like that?'

'Sis, really. You think I'm gonna know that?'

'You're the one that reads all the gossip magazines.'

'Yeah, about young people,' Lana rolled her eyes, thinking for a minute, 'Mum listens to loads of music.'

'Listen,' Emma said, 'I'll hum it and see if we can work out the words.'

Sure enough, Emma began humming. A beautiful sound that soon echoed around them.

'...Angel, you must be talking to an angel...' Lana suddenly interrupted. 'I know the one you mean.'

'Oh My God,' Emma squealed.

'It is the angels. 'They're trying to tell us they're talking to us.'

'But through music? Why not just come down and talk to us face to face?'

'They're not allowed to, are they? Don't you remember some of the stories we've heard?'

Lana shrugged her shoulders.

'A few of the angels are given the chance to come down on very rare occasions, some of them even mate with humans to create Watchers, like our mother did. But they can never stay. That's how Eleanor was cursed, don't you remember any of this?'

'Vaguely,' Lana looked a little embarrassed.

'She was cursed because she fell in love with the man who fathered her own child, Marlene. And so she was forced to stay here, immortal, changing from young to old every single day. Seeing all the people she loved die through the ages. It's so tragic,' Emma murmured.

'Yeah, tragic,' Lana whispered before jumping up on to her feet. 'But why are the angels trying to communicate with us now. Why not just come down and tell us where Eleanor is?'

'Maybe whoever it is up there,' Emma pointed upwards, 'has used up all their travelling time here? Maybe they've been here before and can't come back, so they're doing whatever they can to help us?'

'What if it's not an angel? What it if it's a trap? What if it's a Skull? Or Madge, even?'

'We have to trust our instincts, Lana. What do you feel? Truly, deeply?'

Lana looked around for a moment and bit her bottom lip. 'Like it's really an angel helping us.'

Emma nodded and smiled. 'My thoughts exactly.'

Lana crouched down to her sister and smiled, 'We just have to figure out how to communicate with this person, angel, whatever it is. Come on, we need to get back to the others.'

'Out of the vision?' Emma asked.

Lana nodded, pulling Emma up off the rock.

'But...shouldn't we at least try to find out more?'

'I don't think we are going to be able to?'

'Why not?' asked Emma.

'Because the vision is coming to an end.'

'What makes you sa...' before Emma could finish her sentence, she found herself on the ground with Lana beside her again.

'Hey, you girls alright? Declan shouted from where he and Sammy had been standing earlier.

Lana glanced at her sister.

'Yeah, we had a vision. How come you're still over there?'

'You had a vision?'

Both girls nodded.

'But you only stumbled for a second. You weren't out or anything.'

'We weren't?' Lana replied, confused.

'But we were gone for at least half an hour,' Emma stated.

'Oh well that's new,' Declan said as he bounded over towards them, practically carrying Sammy over the uneven ground.

'I'm okay, thanks Declan. You can put me down now.'

'Oh, sorry mate,' he released his grip on her and she stumbled, just about finding her balance as he reached out for her again.

'Sure?' he grinned.

'Yeah, you know me, klutz dot com,' she chuckled.

'So what happened, girls?' Declan asked. 'You both okay?'

'Yeah,' they said in unison, both grinning.

'Well, what news?' he squinted, shielding his eyes from the brightness of the sunlight through the trees.

'We think we're being helped by an...' Lana gulped and looked at her sister.

'Angel,' finished Emma.

'An angel?' he asked. Tilting his head to one side, he rubbed his chin. 'You sure about that?'

'We think so,' answered Emma before they told him what had happened.

'Okay, so if that's the case, what else did you find out? Any more clues to Eleanor's whereabouts?'

'Only that it might be by the ocean.'

Declan nodded. 'Alright, come on everyone. Let's head back to the car and you can explain what made you come to this conclusion.'

❦   8   ❦

As they drove northwards along the Cabot Trail in Cape Breton, everyone remained quiet, hoping for an elusive clue that would show them the true location of Eleanor and John. Sammy sat listening to her iPod, while Emma and Lana tried to work out why an angel would be helping them. Declan, Marlene and Aria all remained silent, waiting, watching, listening.

Suddenly Sammy screeched, 'Stop.'

Declan slammed on the brakes and pulled over to the side of the road.

'Sammy?' he asked, as she pulled off her headphones and motioned for the others to get out of the van so she, too, could exit.

'I need to go over there,' she pointed to a lone, small tree that stood some fifty metres away from them.

'Oh, okay,' Declan said, pulling on his jacket. 'Wait here guys. I'll go with her.'

He followed her, running across the road until she stood beside this tree that was barely taller than her. He just stood, waiting for her to do her thing.

But she just stood looking at it.

'Are you going to do something?' Declan asked.

Sammy turned towards him and put her finger to her lip, 'Shhhhh.'

Duly told, Declan shut up and waited, watching.

'What do you think she's doing?' asked Aria from the front seat as she and the others had climbed back into the van to try and keep warm.

'I dunno,' Lana replied. 'It's not the same as before. She's not even touching it.'

Suddenly, Sammy nodded her head enthusiastically and pointed in the direction in which they'd just come. She turned back to Declan. 'We've come a little bit too far.'

'That tree told you that?'

Sammy nodded and bounded back towards the vehicle.

Declan simply raised his eyebrows and and followed her.

They got back inside and he turned the van around so they were facing the direction they'd just come.

'Are you sure, Sammy?'

'She told me we missed the turning, about two kilometres back on the right.'

Everyone looked a little quizzical, but Sammy just put her headphones back on and sat back.

'Well, what are we waiting for, Declan? The tree said back, so we go back,' Marlene chuckled as he put his foot on the accelerator and headed down the road.

Lana gently nudged Sammy in the ribs.

She pulled the headphones off her head so they hung around her neck.

'Why was it different this time?' Lana asked quietly.

'What do you mean?'

'You didn't even touch it?'

'The young ones give off so much energy sometimes that you don't need to touch them to communicate with them,' Sammy smiled. 'That one had masses of it. I bet it'll have grown three times as big by this time next year.'

'Oh,' Lana replied.

'How does it know?'

'Know what?' Sammy asked, as she tried to put her headphones back on.

'Where Eleanor is?'

'Oh, he doesn't know that.'

Declan took his foot off the pedal and looked into the rearview mirror, 'Then what does he know? Why are we turning around?'

'Because he knows where the moose are?'

'The moose?' Declan asked.

'Yep.'

'Alrighty then,' Declan smiled, shaking his head before he put his foot back on the accelerator.

A minute later, Sammy tapped him on the shoulder and pointed to the road they'd initially missed.

He nodded and drove off to the right, where a small track led downwards to a clearing in the woods.

'Just park here,' Sammy said as she put her coat back on. 'It would be better if you waited here. I should go alone. Too many of us might scare them off.'

'I'm coming,' Declan said.

'Just you then,' she smiled.

The two of them left the others and set off down into the woods, where they battled masses of underlying giant tree roots to eventually arrive at the side of a body of water.

'There,' Sammy whispered, pointing to movement at the other side of the frozen lake. Silently, a beautiful creature, grey and white in colour with a huge set of impressive antlers, appeared in the distance.

'Wow,' Declan whispered under his breath. 'He's quite something.'

Sammy smiled, 'He is, isn't he? He's quite young, which is why he still has antlers,' she said matter-of-factly. 'They usually shed them in early winter but some of the younger ones keep them for longer. Did you know that?' she asked.

Declan shook his head, clearly impressed.

'I didn't know until now, either. Sometimes, soon as I see them, I seem to know everything needed to know about them. It's incredible. I impress myself at times,' she grinned.

The moose turned its head towards them and Sammy got down on her knees, pulling Declan down beside her. He followed suit until they were both crouching down on the ground.

'It just shows him we're friends.'

'Oh, right.'

After a couple of minutes, the majestic creature began making its way along the shoreline, until it stood about a metre away from them.

'Hey there fella,' Sammy smiled. 'I'd like to talk to you if I may?' she asked him.

The creature tentatively took a couple of steps towards her, while Sammy did the same, until they faced one another.

Declan took a deep breath and watched.

Slowly, Sammy lifted her arm until it rested on the side of the moose's face where she softly stroked his cheek. When he responded by closing his eyes, Sammy smiled and put her other hand on his other cheek. There they stood for about five minutes in absolute silence.

The sound of breathing suddenly brought Declan back to the present moment and he almost jumped out of his skin when he found himself surrounded by even more creatures. He held his breath, not wanting to move a single muscle, but eventually he very slowly turned his head to get a better look. About seven of them stood all around him, all silently watching him.

'Sammy?' he whispered.

But she ignored him until she'd finished communicating with the young moose. Smiling, she dropped one of her hands and continued to rub his other cheek for a moment until the moose bowed its head and stepped backwards.

'Thank you,' she whispered, watching it walk away.

'Sammy?' Declan whispered again.

As she turned, she laughed at his face.

'It's safe, Declan. They've gone.'

Turning around incredibly slowly, Declan was astounded to find the creatures had disappeared without a sound. He relaxed, letting his clenched muscles breathe a sigh of relief.

'There were loads of them, all surrounding me.'

'They were just curious that's all,' Sammy smiled, skipping past him. 'Come on, I'll tell you what happened in the car. I don't want to have to repeat myself twice.'

Declan shook his head and chuckled, 'You don't have to. I already know.'

'Oh yeah, I forgot you could read minds.'

'Well, not animal minds. Only yours, and only when necessary,' he winked.

Sammy smiled and ran on ahead.

'What happened? Do you know where she is?' Lana asked the moment Sammy climbed back in.

She nodded, 'I have a clue,' Sammy replied.

'Well, what is it?' Emma asked.

'The moose travel all around this place, and they see a lot of what goes on. They know when something isn't right and something isn't right at the moment,' she said, the others eagerly looking at her.

'A few months ago, a new house was built right where it shouldn't be. Somewhere normally protected by law. This house isn't like anything they've seen before. It's a bit of a monstrosity.'

'Surely everyone in Nova Scotia must know about it then?' Aria asked.

But Sammy shook he'd head, 'No, it's hidden, secret,' she whispered. 'Maybe even protected by magic. But it's here, it's definitely here.'

'Does the moose know where it is? Can he lead us there?'

Sammy shook her head, 'Not exactly. But he's given me an idea where. It's hidden by many trees and it's very close to the ocean. In the north.'

'I think it's time we changed our mode of transportation, guys,' Declan smiled.

❧ 9 ☙

'Is he ready?' Madge asked Valentine, the oddly dressed young man, who nodded and bowed.

'Very well, the time is coming. I'm assuming Geraldine managed to find her way out of the grounds.

'Yes, Ma'am.'

'Good. You may dispose of Oakley's belongings. Oh and his room is now yours. You may go.'

Valentine looked down, attempting a smile, 'Why thank you, Ma'am,' he said, bowing and retreating out of the room, leaving Madge standing, looking out of the window alone.

'Praxos,' she whispered. 'You have no idea what's coming.'

10

'It's getting dark,' Declan said as he walked out of the boat hire office. 'We're not going to see much tonight. Perhaps we should all get some sleep and continue this at first light?'

'No, Declan that might be too late. Remember the warning, Tempus Edax Rerum? We must continue looking for them.'

'I know, hon. But we can't see anything at night. And you all need some rest, so we'll all be ready for a fight tomorrow. Because I'm sure there is going to be a fight, a big one. Madge isn't going to just let us walk in there and take Eleanor and John, you know? We need to be ready for that.'

'But Declan...'

'No buts, Lana. Rest. Here, I've booked us into this motel. Here's your key. Sammy and Emma are sharing a room with you. Get some sleep. There's some food being delivered in half an hour. Eat, then sleep. We'll head off the second there is light, okay?'

'Okay Declan,' Lana said down-hearted. 'Come on, Sis, Sammy.'

The girls followed her as she walked towards their room. Unlocking the door, she let them in before shutting it behind them.

'So, what do you say we do our own little search tonight?' whispered Lana to the others.

Suddenly there was a bang on the door.

Emma rushed to open it.

Declan stood with his arms crossed, filling the doorframe.

'Are you forgetting that I can hear your thoughts? If you head out of this room alone tonight, there'll be trouble. Do you understand?'

Lana bit her bottom lip, annoyed with herself for getting caught out.

'Do you understand, Lana?'

Eventually, she nodded.

'That goes for you two, as well. Don't let her talk you into doing something you'll regret. If anything happened to you, well, I don't even want to imagine that but just think of your parents. I promised them I'd do everything possible to keep you safe. All of you. You listening?'

'Of course,' Emma answered. 'We'll stay here all night. I promise.'

'Good, now get some shut eye,' he said, smiling slightly at them all before letting Emma close the door.

'Lana, how could you even think of doing something like that?'

She shrugged, 'I just can't bear the thought of Eleanor being holed up with Madge for another night. We still don't know how badly injured she is. I'm just desperate to find her.'

'I know, Sis. I am too. But there are other ways to help, you know. Ways that don't include sneaking out of our room,' Emma grinned.

'Okay, you have my attention,' Lana said rushing to her sister's side on the bed.

'Mine too,' Sammy grinned.

'Have you heard of astral projection?'

Lana sighed loudly.

'No, I'm serious. I've been thinking about it a lot lately. If we keep having these visions that take us places, why can't we control it more? There's no reason why not. We're practically already doing it.'

'Well, I don't know about you, Lana, but I'm intrigued,' Sammy said. 'How do you go about it?'

'Actually, I'm not sure yet but I thought now would as good a time as any to experiment, right?'

'I guess so,' Lana grinned.

'I think we need some serious amount of concentration.

Suddenly, the most enormous stomach gurgle interrupted them all and they all fell about laughing.

'Sorry,' Sammy grinned, holding on to her tummy. 'But I'm starving. I can't think about anything else at the moment but food. I could eat a horse. Well, no I couldn't, me being a vegetarian and all but you know what I mean.'

'Good thing Declan organised some dinner for us then,' Emma smiled as a knock on the door forced her to stand up and go and open it.

'Hey,' she smiled as a friendly middle-aged woman appeared carrying two large trays full of food and drink for them all.

'As ordered by your dad in the room next door,' she smiled. 'Here you go. Enjoy girls!'

'Thank you so much,' Emma giggled as she grabbed the trays and kicked the door shut when the woman had gone.

'Our dad?' Lana rolled her eyes. 'Can you imagine?'

'Actually, Declan would be a pretty cool dad, I think,' Sammy smiled as she grabbed the nearest plate and pulled it towards her.

'Oh no, is that chicken?' she shrieked.

'Oh you must have mine,' Lana said, grabbing the plate and swapping it with the vegetarian pasta. 'Thank God for meat,' she sighed as she sank her teeth into the chicken leg like a cavewoman.

'Ew, Lana. You're so gross.'

'Yes, that's my sister,' Emma added as she sat upright and began spooning the pasta into her mouth.

'Why thanks,' Lana said to the both of them with her mouth open.

'Like I said, gross,' Sammy grinned.

'Hey, this is nice,' Lana said.

'What? The pasta?'

'No, us actually laughing for a change. It feels like a long time ago now.'

'Yeah it does,' Sammy sighed. 'Don't worry, everything is going to be back to normal soon.'

'I hope so. I miss our life in England. I miss studying. I miss mum and dad and the kids and I really miss Diarmuid.'

'Gosh yeah, it's ages since you mentioned him. Haven't you heard from him?'

Emma nodded, 'Of course. I'm just trying not to dwell on the fact that I miss him so much. I'm trying to focus all my energy on finding Eleanor and John. That's what really matters right now, right?'

'Totally,' Lana agreed. 'But I miss everyone as well. And I really wish Barber was here.'

'I still can't believe you're dating a vampire, Lana,' Sammy grinned. 'It's kinda weird.'

'Our whole lives are weird, Sammy.'

'Yeah, good point.'

'Aren't you interested in anyone at Praxos, Sammy? No interesting guy that piques your interest?' Emma asked.

Sammy blushed.

'So there is!' Lana squealed.

But Sammy shook her head, 'There's no guy at the Academy that I'm interested in, I can assure you of that.'

'At home then?' Emma asked.

'Actually, I, er...'

'What, spit it out, Sammy.'

'I'm not exactly into boys.'

'Oh,' Emma said, feeling a little embarrassed.

'You're gay?' screeched Lana. 'Well, that's very cool.'

Sammy's eyes widened and she smiled, 'You really think so?'

'Of course. I hate it when people are made to conform. I think everyone should be who they truly are, and if that means you're a lesbian Watcher, then so be it. Good for you. So, tell me. Who is it that you fancy? I bet it's Ava, she is the most beautiful girl in school, right?'

But Sammy shook her head, 'She is gorgeous but no. Actually it's Cassie.'

'Cassie? Wow, I did not expect that. Does she know? Is she, er, gay too?'

'Actually, we've been seeing each other for a few months now but we wanted to keep it quiet, especially with everything that's beam going on, you know.'

'Sammy, I think that's so lovely,' Emma said as she put her empty plate back on the tray and opened a small bottle of water.

'Thanks guys, it means a a lot. Not many people know the truth about me and it's nice that you're so accepting.'

'I think you'll find everyone at Praxos will be accepting to the real you, Sammy. After all, we're all there because we're different, because we're special, because we're all embracing who we truly are,' Lana said.

'I couldn't have said it better myself,' Emma smiled.

'Do you remember Cassie's tattoo?' Sammy asked.

'Er, no. Why?' Emma asked.

'Esto Quodes. It means Be What You Are. It kind of fits, you know?'

Lana and Emma both smiled.

'Totally. Good for you, Sammy,' Lana grinned as she put down her plate and helped clear the trays out of the way. 'So, about this astral projection stuff. How do we start?'

oOo

IT WAS ALMOST MIDNIGHT, AND THE GIRLS HAD BEEN TRYING FOR hours to get it to work but nothing seemed to do the trick so eventually, they'd given in to their exhaustion and had collapsed on to their beds. Sammy was the first to fall asleep, the gentle sound of her breathing filled the room.

'You still awake, Sis?' asked Emma.

'Yeah. You?'

'Ah funny,' Lana smiled. 'I'm so tired but I can't sleep. Something's stopping me.'

'I know the feeling. Me too,' yawned Emma, as she turned to face her sister.

'I keep thinking about the angel.'

'Yeah, so do I,' Lana replied.

'Do you think it might be our birth mother?'

'I don't know. It would be great, wouldn't it? To finally meet her?'

Emma nodded and moved on to her back, so she faced the ceiling. Lana followed suit until both of them were lying side by side looking upwards.

'Hey, there's that sound again,' Emma murmured as her weary eyes finally closed.

'Yeah, the music,' sighed Lana as she closed hers too.

oOo

'Emma, Emma. Wake up, wake up?' Lana was tugging at her sister's top, and grabbing her shoulder. 'Emma.'

'What? What is it?' Emma sighed, opening her eyes and having to shield them from the bright light.

'Oh man that's bright,' she muttered. 'Is it morning already? It seems like only minutes ago that I closed my eyes.'

'Emma, just look. It's not morning. We're not in the motel room anymore. Look.'

Emma did as she was told and opened her eyes fully, removing her arm from in front of her face.

Slowly, she sat up so she and Lana were sitting beside each other.

'Are we dreaming?' Emma asked.

'Maybe,' Lana replied as they both climbed from the bed.

There was nothing but white all around them, above and below them.

'What is this?' Emma whispered.

'It looks like cotton wool,' Lana said as she held her arms outstretched in front of her to try and feel if anything was really there.

'Are we floating?' Emma asked, not being able to feel the ground beneath her feet was too weird.

'I think we must be dreaming,' Lana said this time. 'Hello?' she asked. 'Is anybody there? God, I sound like someone in a horror movie. So cliched.'

'Hello?' asked Emma.

Lana looked at her and she shrugged her shoulders. 'Well, might as well try it.'

'Is that a door, Sis?' Lana asked as the faint outline of a doorway appeared just a few metres away from them both.

'Hold on to my hand, let's go through together.'

Emma nodded and grabbed hold of her hand. They floated towards it, taking deep breaths before Lana gingerly grabbed onto the handle and pushed the door open.

'Can you see what's on the other side?' Emma whispered.

'Not yet. Should we go through?'

Emma nodded. 'We have to. We don't have a choice.'

Suddenly a deep male voice on the other side answered.

'You always have a choice.'

Lana stopped so abruptly that Emma collided into her.

'Who's that?' she whispered into Lana's ear.

'I dunno,' she replied, fear rolling into her voice.

'Please don't be afraid, Lana. I'm not going to hurt you.'

'Who are you?'

'That's not important right now. What is important is that you accomplish your task.'

'Our task?'

'Yes,' said the voice.

'But what is our task?' Emma asked from behind her.

'To discover the truth and put things to right and live your lives the way they are meant to be lived.'

'That's not really very helpful right now, whoever you are,' Lana huffed.

The man laughed.

'Can we see you. I want to know who you are?'

'Just step through the door,' he insisted.

'Do you think we should?' Lana whispered to her sister who nodded.

'What if it's a trick?'

The man's voice laughed.

'This is no trick. You can believe you're safe right now. You listened to me play before, why not listen to me again?'

'It was you? Playing the harp?' Lana asked as she walked quickly through the doorway.

'It was.'

'But why couldn't you just talk to us?'

'That is not possible.'

. . .

'But you're talking to us now?'

'But you're dreaming,' he answered.

'Oh come on, really?' Lana said loudly.

He laughed again.

'Lana Beth and Emma Jane, the Morgan sisters. Special sisters with special abilities with very special futures ahead of you. Listen to your voices, have faith, be who you truly are, and you will win this battle. But most of all, trust in yourselves. There will be moments that you doubt yourselves and moments when you doubt others but you can do this. You can discover the truth. And when you do, deep down, you will be able to live the lives you've always been destined to live. It is up to you now, girls. We have faith in you.'

Suddenly, the white mist began to lift. Emma and Lana watched as a handsome black man began to walk away.

'Wait! Don't go. We don't even know who you are?'

The man turned and smiled, 'That's not important, not anymore. What matters the most is you,' he said and as he turned the white mist began to thicken again.

'But what if we need your help? How can we reach you?'

'I will be watching but you can do this without me. Trust in yourselves,' the voice whispered.

Before he drifted away, they watched as his figure seemed to morph into someone else but all they caught a glimpse of was long blonde hair just moments before the person disappeared completely.

11

Lana woke up, stretching out her limbs beneath the bed covers, before she realised she was still fully dressed. Turning, she saw Emma was still sleeping soundly, so she tiptoed out of the bed and walked towards the window. Opening the curtains, she noticed it was still quite dark outside.

'Lana?' asked a voice from the other bed. 'What time is it?'

'Morning Sammy. It's just after five.'

'Wow, that's crazy early,' she said, turning back over.

'Not so fast, Sammy. We've got to get up and get ready to head out soon.'

'Oh yeah,' Sammy murmured. 'I just need some...'

Before she could finish her sentence there was a gentle tap on the motel door.

'Girls?' said the sweet voice of Marlene. 'It's time to get up.'

'Lana moved swiftly to the door and opened it, 'Hey Marlene.'

'Oh you're up already.'

'Kind of. I slept in my clothes,' Lana smiled. 'But I woke up ten minutes ago. Had the weirdest dream.'

'Morning,' said a muffled voice from beneath the bed covers.

'Morning Emma,' Marlene said. 'I brought you hot tea and coffee,' she placed the three takeaway cups on the sideboard and turned to walk out. 'Declan said we're heading out in fifteen minutes,'

'Okay, thanks Marlene. We'll be ready. Thanks for the drinks.'

Marlene smiled and closed the door behind her.

'Get up sleepy heads,' Lana said to both girls as they stretched out and rubbed their eyes.

'Here, Marlene brought us coffee, Sammy. And Em, a nice cup of green tea. I really don't know how you drink that stuff,' she said, handing her the paper cup.

'It's good for you,' Emma muttered as she climbed out of bed and grabbed the cup, holding it in her hands to warm up before she took a sip.

'Mmmm, delicious,' she smiled. 'Oh, I had the weirdest dream last night,' she murmured as she put the cup down and started to put her shoes on.

'Yeah? Me too. Really weird. You were there,' Lana replied.

'Oh yeah? You were in mine too. It was like we were in heaven or something.'

Lana immediately put her coffee cup down on the bedside table and gazed at her sister, 'Was it all white?' she asked.

Emma looked up from tying up her boot laces and stopped, 'Y... eah and there was this door...'

'And a man's voice...' Lana interrupted.

'That told us to fight and be prepared to live out our destinies...' Emma continued.

'Before disappearing and turning into someone else,' Lana finished.

Sammy sat, her mouth dropped open as she listened to the two girls describe the exact same dream.

'It wasn't a dream?' Emma asked as Lana shook her head. 'A vision?'

'That was the angel that's helping us?'

'It must've been,' Lana replied. 'But who was it?'

'And why did he change?'

'Woah woah woah,' Sammy finally interrupted. 'What's going on?' she asked as there was another knock at the door.

'You ready, girls?' Declan asked from outside of the motel room.

'Oops, just two secs,' shouted Sammy as she rushed to the bathroom along with the sisters, to brush their teeth.

oOo

'AND THEN HE CHANGED INTO WHAT LOOKED LIKE A WOMAN with long blonde hair.'

'And that's all you saw?' Declan asked, his eyebrows almost meeting in the middle.

Lana and Emma both nodded while he deftly took the boat out of the dock.

'It's odd, I'll give you that,' he said. 'But it is possible it was just a dream.'

'That we both had? At the same time? I don't think so,' Emma pondered. 'I believe it was a vision. My gut tells me so.'

'Mine too,' Lana said. 'That guy, girl, angel whatever it was telling us to trust ourselves.'

'Didn't you trust yourselves before?' Aria asked from where she sat beside them as the boat cut through the water.

'Well, I guess I had my moments,' Lana smirked.

'And you, Emma?' she asked.

Emma turned away and shook her head.

'No?' Aria asked again.

'Not since... since...' Emma stuttered before clearing her throat, 'Before Sthenelaus. I guess I've been second guessing myself ever since I k...k...killed him.'

Declan stole a glance at Lana. Both smiled. It was the first time she'd openly said it out loud like that. A huge step forward. But neither said anything.

'But since we got to Nova Scotia, I don't know. I feel different. Stronger, somehow. Like being closer to finding Eleanor and John,' she added, looking across at Aria, '...is giving me strength. I think whoever that angel was helped me to see that.'

'That's great,' Marlene stepped in. 'I'm all for anyone helping us to find my mother,' she smiled.

'I keep forgetting that Eleanor is your mum,' Sammy interjected. 'Even though you look alike,' she blushed, 'and sound the same. Basically, I'm just pretty lame.'

'Don't be silly,' Marlene smiled. 'We're so focussed on finding them, we kind of forget these things. It's okay. Focus is good.'

Sammy smiled back at the beautiful young blonde woman as the boat finally made it's way out into the open ocean.

'Right, keep your eyes peeled folks. She's got to be around here somewhere.'

They all stepped away from one another, each taking up a position on the edge of the boat, their eyes focussing out towards the hundreds of trees along the shoreline and higher up on the rockier outcrops.

For twenty minutes, nobody said a thing until Sammy pointed and yelled out, 'Over there.'

They all rushed back towards Declan and she pointed again to where she'd seen something a little unusual. Declan took the binoculars to his eyes and scoured the landscape.

'It's an old wooden house, looks a bit dilapidated. Doesn't really look like something that was built recently. Oh, but hang on,' he added. Looks like there's something just beside it, but it's hidden somehow. Ouch,' he suddenly said, dropping the binoculars to the floor of the boat. He doubled over, hands covering his ears.

'What is it, Declan?' Aria and Marlene both bent down to help him.

'There's something blocking me,' he cried. 'The pain, it's intense. C...can't... can't...' suddenly he fell in a heap to the floor.

'Do you hear anything?' Aria asked Marlene as they tried to sit him upright but she shook her head.

'No, nothing. Let's get him below deck.'

With the help of the others, they managed to get him below, where they propped him up against some pillows on a rickety old bed down there. His face continued to crumple up in pain.

'I think we should go back,' Marlene whispered.

'No,' Declan urged. 'It's just some sort of barrier. Now we know we're in the right place, we can't go back,' he said, sweat dripping down his forehead. 'It's not like it's gonna kill me, right?' he tried to joke.

'Very funny Declan,' Lana said as she held a bottle of water to his lips.

'Where's Emma?' he asked at the exact moment the sound of a splash came from the side of the boat.

'Gone for a swim?' Lana suggested, biting her bottom lip.

'Oh My God,' Sammy screeched, rushing back towards the steps.

'No use panicking,' Lana said. 'She did it on purpose. She knows she's the only one who can get close enough to investigate. She'll be okay. I have every faith in her,' she smiled.

'I can't... I can't... hear her thoughts. Or any of yours, for that matter. This... this thing is stopping it all.'

'Shhhh, don't try to talk. Just try and control it,' Aria said. 'Remember the breathing techniques you always use for everybody else? Well, now's the time to use them on yourself, okay, Dec?' she asked.

Declan winced and tried to chuckle, nodding. 'Yeah, yeah,' he muttered under his breath.

'It'll help with the pain,' she urged.

While Aria and Marlene both helped Declan to try and get the pain under control, Sammy and Lana headed back up top to see if they could catch a view of Emma or anyone else, for that matter anywhere near Madge's place.

'See anything?' asked Lana as Sammy peered through the binoculars Declan had dropped. But she shook her head.

'No, nothing. I can't even get a good look at the house, can you? It's weird, it's like it's not even there anymore.'

'It's probably got some kind of spell on it. Madge is probably working with a witch - or a few of them. And there must be guards protecting her. I mean, she had loads of Skulls protecting her in England. I just don't see any of them though,' Lana replied, scouring the view in the distance. 'I wonder how Emma's doing.'

Beneath the surface, Emma enjoyed the peaceful sounds of the water before deftly climbing out onto the beach closest to the house. Shivering, she concentrated hard on warming herself up, thankful for the wetsuit the boat hire company had lent them. It was much easier to dry a wetsuit with her warming skills, than jeans and a jumper. Hiding behind a huge rock in the sand, she waited until she was fully dry before she carefully stepped out and looked around at her surroundings. It was the most beautiful location, a small beach covered in pieces of driftwood, both massive and small. She found a long, strong piece of wood which would double up as protection should she need it, and quietly clambered over the rocks and wood until she stood at the top end of the beach.

Still no sign of any Skulls, Emma looked back towards the boat for a moment, nodding and briefly waving to let the others know she was alright. She was almost certain they'd be watching.

Sure enough, Lana and Sammy were doing just that.

'She's on the beach,' Sammy whispered, handing the binoculars to Lana. 'Looks okay to me.'

'I figured she would be,' Lana replied as she focussed on her sister as she turned away from the ocean and began walking up towards the house. 'I wish I was there with her though. It's so unfair she can swim in freezing temperatures and I can't,' she tutted.

'You have your own skills,' Sammy smiled. 'I bet Emma can't jump from crazy heights like you can.'

Lana smirked, 'No, that's all me,' she winked. 'Not that it's doing me much good here though.'

'What about astral projection?' Sammy suggested. 'I know it didn't work last night, but if you tried again now? Maybe it would work, I dunno,' she shrugged. 'Might be worth a try.'

'Sammy, you're a genius. Maybe the angel will help me do it?' she almost squealed, clapping her hands together.

'But how are you going to communicate with the angel?' Sammy asked as they both walked to the back of the boat where she could sit down and focus.

'I have a feeling he'll hear me. All I need to do is... ask,' she smiled and closed her eyes.

Sure enough, moments later when Sammy tried to get Lana's attention, it seemed that, although her body was there, her mind most certainly wasn't.

'Hey,' said Marlene, startling her.

'How's Declan?' Sammy asked.

'I'm afraid he's still in rather a lot of pain. What are you up to? Have you seen Emma yet?'

Sammy nodded, 'Yeah, she's just got to the beach and is headed up towards the house now.'

'Lana are you alright?' Marlene asked, sitting down beside her.

'Erm, I don't really think she's there, Marlene,' Sammy said, shyly.

'What do you mean?'

'I think she might have astral projected over there.'

'Astral projection? How on earth has she done that? I didn't know that was one of her abilities,' she said, shocked.

Sammy swallowed loudly, 'She and Emma were trying to get it to work last night but couldn't and then, after this angel thing, well, she figured if she just asked him, that he might help her achieve it. Judging by the state of her, I'm guessing he did.'

Marlene and Sammy both turned to look at Lana who sat upright on the seat. Although her eyes were closed, they noticed rapid eye movement beneath the lids.

'Something's definitely going on,' Marlene whispered. 'Can I have the binoculars?'

Sammy nodded and handed them to Eleanor's daughter, who immediately jumped up and headed back to the front of the vessel where she stood looking for evidence that Lana had indeed astral projected to Emma's location.

Sure enough, there she was. A carbon copy of Lana, running along the beach.

'Sammy, I'm going to need a wetsuit,' she yelled.

🏵 12 🏵

'Emma wait up,' Lana tried to say without actually shouting out loud.

'Huh? Lana? How in the world did you get here?' Emma whispered, turning back and running towards her sister. But you're bone dry? How...'

'It's not really me. I mean, it's me, but not me. I'm not making any sense at all, am I?'

Emma shook her head and tried to grab her sister's hand. When her own hand went straight through her, her eyes widened and she grinned.

'You did it,' she tried not to squeal. 'Astral projection. How on earth?'

'Well that's the thing, it wasn't really me... I just asked the angel to help me do it and, voila, here I am. Cool huh?'

'Totally cool, but come on. We might not have much time. Let's go.'

'Oh yeah, Eleanor,' Lana said, as they both turned back and headed up the beach, to where the sand, driftwood and rocks met a multitude of trees.

'This is where Sammy would be useful,' Emma whispered as they went from one tree to the next, hiding behind each one and scouring the area before moving on.

'It's weird that there doesn't seem to be anyone around here.

Surely she must have loads of Skulls for protection?' Lana murmured when they stopped to catch their breath. 'Quite a few of them jumped into that weird wormhole so they should be here - and Stan,' she practically spat his name out. 'He'll be here for sure. So be careful, Sis. It's not like they can hurt me like this but you, well...'

'I know, Lana. I'll be careful.'

As they continued to rush through the trees, neither girl never once let her guard down. Soon, they were standing in front of a massive, rather ugly house, with mirrored glass everywhere - which camouflaged the property from the outside world. From a distance, you could barely see it. All you could see were trees.

'Right, how do we get in?' Emma whispered as they tiptoed, crouching down for safety.

'Over there,' came a voice behind them.

'Jesus, Marlene. You frightened the life out of me. You must be freezing cold. Emma...'

'I'm on it,' Emma replied, walking up to Marlene, preparing to use her core heat to put some warmth back into Marlene's body but the woman shook her head.

'No need, thank you Emma. It didn't affect me.'

'Oh?'

'I've been around for quite some time, you see. I'm not quite immortal, but I'm quite often immune to things, like extreme temperatures. Thank you though, you're very kind.'

Emma blushed as Marlene walked past them both, 'It looks like there's an entryway over there. Follow me.'

The three of them surreptitiously crept over to the door where Marlene confidently picked the lock in a matter of seconds.

'Wow,' Lana whispered, clearly impressed. 'She's amazing,' she mouthed to Emma behind her.

'This is too easy though,' Marlene said, looking back. 'This place should be teeming with Skulls. I'm afraid we might be at the wrong place.' Her face appeared concerned as they pushed open the door. All three of them were crouched, ready for attack, but the attack didn't come.

'What's going on?' Lana whispered as they walked in and looked around at the very stylish, contemporary kitchen all done out in white and chrome.

'Do you think this house belongs to someone else? Maybe it's a cover?' Marlene whispered.

'The old wooden shack next door,' Emma cried. 'I bet they're in there,' she turned and the others immediately followed behind her as they rushed out of the house.

Creeping closer to the old property, the sound of a small motor getting closer distracted them. The three girls turned to look down towards the beach where they saw Declan, Aria and Sammy all climb out of a little dinghy and run up towards them. Declan was clearly no longer in pain.

They waited for the three of them to arrive, before Declan asked, 'What's going on? Anything?'

All three girls shook their heads, 'Nothing. The house seems to be empty. We thought maybe it's just a cover for the shack next door?' Marlene said. 'You okay?'

He nodded, 'The pain suddenly stopped. I figured maybe you'd found her.'

But Lana shook her head. We didn't do anything. Only opened the door to the kitchen, saw something wasn't quite right and came back out again. This is too weird.'

'We need to check out next door,' Emma whispered. 'I have a horrible feeling about it.'

'In that case, let's move out,' Declan said as he motioned for them all to stay behind him.

The sound of muffled voices brought them to a standstill and Declan held up his hand to make them stay still.

He looked around for a moment and pointed to Marlene, Sammy and Lana, before indicating that they go together and he'd lead the others in the other direction. Marlene nodded and they headed around the back of the wooden shack, while Declan and the others headed towards the side of the house.

The muffled voices didn't get louder or quieter.

'What is that?' Emma whispered to Aria.

'I'm not sure,' she replied, 'but it doesn't seem to be coming from the house, it seems to be coming from out here.'

Declan turned back and lifted his head, listening, 'You're right. 'It's like it's the trees or something. We need Sammy.'

The trio made their way towards the back of the house where Marlene was leading Sammy and Lana.

'Anything?' he asked. They all shook their heads, just as Marlene gently pushed the back door, which was ajar, wide open. Inside was nothing but a single table and a small broken glass bottle.

'There are voices outside but they seem to be coming from the trees, Sammy. I think we need your expertise, hon.'

Sammy nodded as they all retreated back, following the gentle muffled sounds. She looked all around, upwards and downwards before deciding on a particular tree which stood closer to the house than any of the others. Slowly, she circled it before carefully placing her hand on it's trunk. A moment later, she placed her other one beside it. Closing her eyes, she started to hum. But after a second, she was propelled backwards, leaving her stunned and a little winded on the ground.

'Sammy!' yelled Declan who immediately rushed to her side and picked her up.

'You alright, mate?' he asked.

Just as she began to nod, the sound of whirring blades interrupted them. All stopped to listen as the approaching noise became closer and closer.

'Madge?' asked Lana but Declan shook his head and smiled.

'No, it's our guys. Giovanni and the troops.'

Suddenly, a massive chinook helicopter hovered above them and a large number of what appeared to be soldiers were dropping from it using long ropes, landing just metres from them.

Soon, they were surrounded.

'Declan?' came a voice in the distance.

'Giovanni?' Declan replied, shouting above the sound of the whirring blades as it began to move away from them all.

'Thanks for the heads-up,' Giovanni said, 'We got here as fast as we could. Where are they?'

'That's the thing. They don't appear to be here,' Declan replied, somewhat baffled. 'But, there's something going on in these trees here. Like muffled voices or something. Well, it did sound like muffled voices. It seems to have stopped now. Listen,' he said as everyone quietened down for a moment. Sure enough, the sounds had stopped.

Giovanni nodded.

'We're just trying the gentle approach,' Declan said, looking down at Sammy who was still in his arms.

Giovanni stepped backwards and motioned for his troops to hold still while Declan returned Sammy to the ground.

'What happened?' he asked quietly looking down at her.

'She's a little unsure of us,' she whispered back. 'She's had some pretty horrible experiences these last few weeks.'

'So this is the right place then,' Declan asked.

'Definitely,' Sammy replied. 'Can I try again?'

'Are you sure you're alright, mate?'

Sammy nodded and turned back to look at the tree, 'I'm okay. She's just a bit shell-shocked, that's all.'

Declan nodded and stepped back, 'Over to you then.'

Sammy took a particularly deep breath and stepped forward, once more placing both hands on the side of the tree.

This time, she rested her forehead on it as well and gently made some whispering sounds. After a couple of seconds, she breathed in and began to hum. The ethereal sound soon echoed throughout the woods, making the Watcher soldiers all look around in wonder as some of the other trees began to sway even though there was no wind to cause it.

Sammy suddenly gasped and tears began to fall down her cheeks.

'Sammy? Sammy, are you alright?' asked Emma, who had slowly approached her friend and was looking at her with concern.

'Some of them have been hurt pretty badly,' Sammy answered. 'Some of them are dead. Find the dead trees, and you'll find them. That's what they're telling me. Find the dead trees and you'll find who you're looking for. Oh God,' she whispered gently stroking the trees. 'How could she do this to them? How could she hurt them like this?'

'It's okay Sammy, let's find them. Can you help us find them? Help us find the dead trees?' Declan asked as he helped her step away from the tree.

Slowly, she nodded, the tears continuing to fall down her cheeks.

'Of course,' she cried. 'But there's lots.'

'Over there,' she pointed. 'The first is over there. You'll find a body inside.'

Declan and Giovanni both ran towards the tree she was pointing at. Sure enough, the tree was either dying or already dead. They looked at it, stumped and then walked around it. Giovanni scratched his head.

'Where? Where is she?'

'Inside, Giovanni,' Sammy cried, falling to her knees. 'The body is inside.'

'Oh God,' Declan said loudly as he clawed at the bark, unable to get in.

'No, you'll have to go in from the top,' Sammy added, getting back up to her feet. With a sudden burst of energy, she ran towards it, grabbed the lowest branch, swung until her feet caught the next branch upwards and continued until she was able to peer down into the hollow middle of the tree.

'No,' she screamed.

'Help get her down,' Declan shouted to some of the soldiers. 'We need to do exactly what she did to every single dead tree around this house. Get up there and find what's inside. Just be careful. We don't know if any are booby-trapped.'

When Emma and Lana began to move towards the trees, Declan boomed at them both.

'No!' he yelled. 'Not you. You stay put. I'm not risking you being blown up or something. We don't know what's down there.'

Sammy, who had been helped back down by a huge soldier with very gentle hands, was shaking her head. 'No, Declan. There's no trap. Just the bodies.'

'Are you absolutely certain, Sammy?'

She nodded again. 'Absolutely certain. There is no danger here, nothing but bodies, some barely alive.'

He nodded to the troops until almost every tree in the vicinity had a couple of soldiers climbing up it.

❧ 13 ❧

'How many?' asked Declan thirty minutes later.

'Seventeen so far,' answered the lead soldier as all the bodies were carefully placed in body bags and lined next to one another on the ground.

'All dead?' he whispered and the soldier nodded in response.

'But there's still more.'

Declan looked across at his colleagues and watched as more soldiers continued to hoist the people out of the trees.

'We've got a live one,' shouted a voice from further afield.

'And another,' said a second soldier.

Declan and the girls rushed over to see and lend a hand.

'Is it Eleanor?' Emma asked, but the man shook his head. 'A young male.'

As the unconscious man was pulled out of the tree, Lana did a double take.

'I've seen him before,' she said, stepping backwards. 'He's a Skull,' she said loudly.

Declan immediately rushed to her side and looked down at the man who was carefully laid out of the floor.

'And he's alive?' asked Declan. The soldier leaned forward, taking his pulse he nodded.

'Barely, but yes,' he said.

'Medic!' Declan yelled as the medic appeared by his side.

'I can help,' voiced Emma.

'Emma, he's a Skull,' Lana spat.

'Yes and he's been left for dead. Why?' Emma asked. 'Maybe he turned on her or something?'

'He's still a person and deserves to be treated,' Marlene appeared by their side. 'Besides, we need to know what happened here and hopefully he can help us.'

'Where's the other live one?' asked Declan, as he stood back up and looked around.

'We're just pulling him out,' said Giovanni who had been hoisted up the tree to get a good look. 'It's another male. About thirty years old.'

'John?' came a voice from further away.

'Wait, Aria. We don't know...' Declan said as she rushed past him, almost knocking him over.

As the man was very carefully laid to rest on the forest floor, Aria let out a deep groan.

'Oh My God, John. It's really you,' she cried, as she gently caressed the man's face.

'Will he make it?' she whispered.

'Medics, get down here now,' Giovanni instructed. 'This man is one of ours and he needs immediate attention.'

'Wait,' yelled Emma. 'Let me help. I can help him,' she said, pushing the others out of the way in her rush to get to Aria's side.

'Aria, please,' she said. 'I need some room.'

Reluctantly, Aria moved out of her way, but continued to hold steadily onto her man's hand.

'Please do everything you can to save him, Emma.'

Emma nodded and placed both her hands on John's chest. Closing her eyes, she focussed all of her energy on the near-dead Watcher who had been in the Sophokles grasp for years. Her hands began to glow a deep red, and a faint golden aura appeared to hover above them both.

'Please, please don't die John,' Aria sobbed beside them. 'Please come back to me.'

Emma opened her eyes, noticing a commotion in the

distance. She glanced at Declan and motioned for him to go and see what was happening, before she closed her eyes again and continued to do all she could to bring John back from the brink of death.

Very slowly, she began to feel a stronger heartbeat beneath her fingers and so she released her hands and let them hover over his chest, moving them along his torso until they stopped over his head.

'He has a head injury, Aria,' Emma whispered, 'But his heart is strong. He needs to get to our hospital pronto.'

Aria nodded as Emma slowly stood up. Soldiers immediately rushed to his side and lifted his body onto a stretcher, carrying him to the nearby truck.

'Go with him,' Emma said to Aria who was beside herself with tears. 'He needs you now.'

Aria could barely talk so she merely nodded and rushed after her fiancee.

'What's going on?' Emma asked Lana as she walked quickly down towards the commotion.

Lana turned to look at her sister before she pulled her into a deep hug.

'What? What is it?' she asked, confused.

'It's Eleanor. They found Eleanor.'

Emma gasped, 'Is she alive?'

Lana nodded.

'And conscious?'

'No.'

'Let me see her,' Emma cried, pushing people out of the way as she tried to get to Eleanor. 'Please move, I can help, let me get to her.'

As the crowd began to open a little, Emma saw Declan stand up from the ground with Eleanor in his arms. The medics were trying to get to her but Declan was looking through the crowd trying to locate Emma.

He shook his head at the other doctors, 'No,' he said firmly. 'There's only one person who can heal her,' Emma heard him say.

'Emma?' he croaked as he climbed over large tree roots to get to her.

'It's Eleanor,' he cried. 'We found Ellie,' emotion clearly over-coming him momentarily.

'Put her down here,' Emma instructed, pointing to a clearing in the woods.

Doing exactly as he was told, Declan very gingerly placed their Guardian on the ground, careful to hold her head while Lana rushed over, taking off her coat and folding it so it could be used as a pillow.

'We've got you Ellie,' Declan whispered, remaining on his knees while Emma got to work.

Just like before, she placed her hands over her heart and focussed all her energy on healing the woman who had changed her life.

Her hands, which moved up and down the woman's torso, glowed a deep red before turning golden, the aura above them both getting stronger and stronger.

For a second, Lana noticed her sister grimace as her hands stopped just below the woman's heart.

'What is it, Sis?' Lana whispered.

But Emma just briefly shook her head and continued with her eyes closed, not caring about anything but healing Eleanor.

'Emma?' Declan said quietly.

But Emma shook her head again before whispering, 'Just a minute.'

Declan nodded and looked up at Lana before he realised they were surrounded by the rest of the soldiers. Giovanni stood quietly beside Lana while Marlene stood some distance behind them all.

He heard a faint sob coming from her direction and motioned for her to come closer but she couldn't. Not yet.

Instead, he returned his full attention to the Guardian of the Watchers and the young woman who was giving it her all to heal her.

Suddenly, miraculously, Eleanor took a deep breath in.

Emma immediately stopped what she was doing, 'Eleanor?' she whispered.

Declan's eyes opened wide as Eleanor's lashes fluttered slightly before her breath seemed to return to normal.

'Is she alright, mate?' he asked Emma whose hands had returned to hover just below Eleanor's heart.

'I...I... I'm not sure. But her heartbeat is much steadier now. I think if we can get her to our hospital quickly, she can be saved.'

Declan nodded and looked up towards Giovanni, who was already organising her transportation.

Marlene was nowhere to be seen.

✳ 14 ✳

'**M**arlene!' Declan yelled some time later, once the bodies had been removed and the three patients were en-route to the nearest Praxos hospital.

'Mate, where are you?' he shouted as he wandered through the trees that had, just a few hours earlier, been full of bodies.

Stumbling over a small tree stump, he steadied himself. Suddenly, he felt like he was able to pick up on someone's thoughts so he looked up and out towards the ocean. There, in the boat they had used to find the house, was Marlene. She sat with her back towards him, looking out across the vast blue blanket of water.

Declan breathed a sigh of relief and walked down towards the beach.

Sammy sat, leaning against a large piece of driftwood, holding a pebble in her hand.

'You alright, Sammy?' Declan asked as he sat down beside her.

'Yeah,' she muttered.

'You been keeping an eye on Marlene?'

'I was worried about her,' Sammy said as she threw the pebble across the water, watching it skip twice above it before it sank.

'You and me both, mate.'

'Can't you read her mind?' Sammy asked, looking sideways at him.

'She's a hard one to read,' he smiled. 'She can shut me out. Not many people can do that. Yours, on the other hand, are usually much easier. But since earlier on, I'm having some difficulty with reading anyone's'.

She raised her eyebrows.

'I picked up on something faint, which is what made me look out towards the boat.'

Sammy nodded, this time picking up a long thin piece of driftwood which she used to draw in the sand.

'Do you think she's going to be alright?'

'I hope so,' Declan said, 'But we'll have to wait and see what happens at the hospital. Eleanor is a strong Guardian and she's always been a fighter.'

'And Marlene?'

Declan sighed, 'She hasn't seen her mother for a very long time. It must've been pretty awful to see her like that. But I reckon she'll be fine. She just needs a bit of time to herself.'

'Declan?' came a voice in his head.

He frowned and looked around.

'Declan? It's me, Marlene.'

'Actually Sammy, she seems to be communicating with me.'

Sammy looked at him quizzically as he tapped the side of his head and pointed out towards Marlene.

'I know you can hear me. I just needed a few moments to myself.'

Declan smiled.

'I'll take the boat back. Don't worry, I'll be fine. I'll meet you back at the motel.'

'Come on, mate,' Declan said, standing up and holding out his hand to Sammy. 'Time to go.'

'But what about Madge?' she asked.

Declan sighed, 'Honestly, I reckon she's long gone.'

'Don't you think it's a bit strange though?' Sammy asked. 'Killing all those people and just leaving?'

Declan shrugged. 'Let's worry about her later. For now, let's concentrate on Eleanor. We've got her back and that's all that matters.'

Sammy took his hand and pulled herself up, 'Yeah I guess you're right.'

❧ 15 ❧

Two weeks later

'Can you believe it's finally over?' Diarmuid asked Emma as they sat across from each other in the Praxos Academy's main dining room, their hands intertwined, empty plates sitting between them.

'Thankfully,' she sighed. 'Now we can carry on, finish our studies and move on with our lives.'

Diarmuid raised his eyebrows, 'That sounds a bit ominous.'

Grinning, Emma squeezed his hand, letting her core temperature increase somewhat so that their hands glowed pink. 'Not really. Have you thought about it though?'

'About what?'

'Your future?'

'Mine or ours?' he grinned as he watched her fingers stroke his, the faint aura glowing stronger with every breath she took.

'Ours?' she whispered and he smiled.

'I was hoping we would carry on at Praxos together. Maybe become healers here?'

Emma grinned, 'Is that what you want? To continue working here in London?'

He chuckled, 'Don't you?'

'Honestly, I just know this is what I want to do. With you, either here or well, anywhere. But I know I want to heal.'

'So medical school then?'

'I guess so.'

'Can we do that here? Can we carry on studying that here?' he asked.

Emma nodded, 'I spoke to Declan about it. We can continue to study both here and at the nearby University of Westminster. He said he can arrange everything for us both if that's what we want.'

'Oh My God, Em, that's amazing. If that's what you really want, then I'm all for it.'

'Of course it's what I really want. I know I have a future here and I know my future is with you. It's kind of the right thing to do.'

Diarmuid suddenly stood up and walked around to her side of the table. He pulled her up off her feet and in towards him, before moving in for a deep, passionate kiss.

'Woah guys get a room already,' said a familiar voice from the doorway.

Turning, they both grinned at the sight of Lana, hand in hand with Barber.

'Hey Sis,' Emma sighed. 'All okay?'

'We just came to tell you. It's happened. She's...'

'Awake?' asked Emma, her eyes rounding with expectation.

Lana smiled and nodded.

'Word is getting round school that Eleanor woke up this morning.'

Emma clapped her hands together and immediately pulled Diarmuid towards the door.

'Not so fast,' Barber said. 'Declan told me to stop anyone from trying to go and see her. She's still very weak and will need time to compose herself.'

'Of course,' Emma replied, slowing herself down.

'He's right,' Diarmuid added, 'Let's go for a walk. Maybe she'll be ready to see you later on?'

Emma nodded. 'What are you guys doing?' she turned towards her sister.

'Not much,' Lana said, trying to sound bored.

'Oh really?' Emma asked. 'Not much, eh? You're lying through your teeth, Sis.'

'Hey,' Lana said, gently punching Emma on the shoulder. 'You always know when something's up. Jeeze.'

'You're just so easy to read, Lana. So, what are you really up to?'

Barber grinned.

'Barber is going to let me drive his motorbike.'

Emma's brow creased, 'Really? Is that safe? What if you fall off?'

Lana shook her head, 'I'm a Watcher, Sis. So what if I do? Don't worry, I won't drive too fast,' she said crossing her fingers behind her back.

'Just be careful,' Emma sighed. 'I don't want to be treating you in a hospital bed tonight. Watch out for her, Barber.'

'Of course. I'll guard her with my life.'

He and Lana both laughed as they turned to walk out.

'Does that really mean anything when you're a vampire?' asked Emma, shaking her head. 'That girl is crazy.'

'Yep,' Diarmuid replied, 'But she wouldn't be Lana if she wasn't.'

'I know, I know.'

'Has she decided what she's going to do yet?'

'You mean once we've finished our studies here?' she asked.

Diarmuid nodded.

'I've tried asking her about it but haven't really had a serious answer yet. I guess she's still thinking about it. I just hope she takes it seriously.'

'I'm sure she will, Em. Don't worry about her. She'll always be able to look after herself.'

'Yeah I know, but I do worry that she'll wind up making a decision based on what Barber's doing, and not on what she really should be doing.'

'You sound like your mum,' he grinned as he casually draped his arm across her shoulders and led her out of the dining room.

'I always was the serious one.'

'Hey Emma,' came a voice out of the darkness across the other side of the great hall. 'I heard Eleanor woke up. Great job!'

'Thanks Rupert. Hopefully we can all see her soon and get back to normal.'

'Normal? What's normal around here,' he joked, patting Diarmuid on the back as they crossed paths. 'Have a fun Sunday.'

'You too, mate,' Diarmuid replied with a grin.

'Diarmuid, you have a phone call in the main office. It's your mum,' said Wilbur, who seemed to have appeared out of nowhere.

'Oh, that's odd. I wonder why she didn't ring my mobile?'

'She said it's switched off,' Wilbur said, shaking his head at the teenager.

'Oh right,' I've not needed to charge it much since you got back,' he smiled at Emma. 'I'll catch up with you in a minute.'

'Okay,' she replied. 'I'm going to see if I can have a word with Declan. See you by the infirmary?'

'Sure,' Diarmuid leaned forward and kissed her quickly on the lips.

Wilbur cleared his throat impatiently.

oOo

APPROACHING THE INFIRMARY, EMMA STOOD QUIETLY BY THE door looking in through the window. She smiled at the sight of Eleanor sitting up in the bed. After a week's treatment at the Praxos Hospital in Boston, Eleanor was flown home. Even though she remained unconscious, she was deemed well enough for the journey.

Since she'd returned to London, Emma (along with a number of other skilled Watchers) had treated Eleanor every morning and evening, hoping that she would soon regain consciousness

Today was that day.

Tapping on the door, she waited a moment before pushing it open and peering inside.

'Can I come in?' she asked Declan who was standing beside the door, quietly talking to Theodore, the gentle Scottish giant who was a renowned healer in their world.

'Emma, how yer doin, lassie? Yer've been doing a fine job with Ellie here.'

Emma smiled as he gently hugged her.

'But something's wrong?' she asked, looking from his concerned face to the very same expression on Declan's.

Both nodded.

'What is it? Is she going to be alright?'

'It's her memory. She can't remember a thing.'

'What? Nothing? No idea where Madge is now? Nothing about what happened?'

Both men shook their heads, 'That and more,' Theodore added.

'She doesn't know who we are, Emma.'

Emma gasped as she listened to Declan tell her about the extreme memory loss.

'But what do the doctors say?'

'We've had some of the best Praxos neurologists in to see her and they're all baffled.'

'Maybe it has something to do with the stabbing?' Emma suggested.

'Aye lassie, we thought of that too,' Theodore said.

'But that's another thing that's baffling the doctors,' Declan interrupted.

'There's a very slight scar just below her heart but no evidence of scar tissue beneath it.'

Emma remembered when she'd first healed Eleanor two weeks earlier, she'd picked up on a strange feeling in the same place.

Nodding, she said, 'Yeah, I kind of picked up on something odd there when we found her.'

'We're assuming Madge treated her.'

'But why? If she wanted her dead? It makes no sense.'

'Exactly what we're thinking. There's something not quite right here,' said Declan.

'But at least she's safe now,' Emma pondered, looking in between the two of them at Eleanor who sat upright, sipping at a glass of water that was being held by a nurse.

'So she doesn't know who you are? Not even you, Declan?'

Declan shook his head, 'Not a thing.'

'And Marlene?'

Again, both men shook their heads.

'Not even Wilbur?'

'Nope.'

'Can I try and talk to her?' she whispered.

The men looked at each other and both shrugged.

'Anything is worth a try at this point,' Declan said, moving to one side so she could walk in between them.

Emma took a deep breath and slowly walked towards the bed in which Eleanor was tucked into.

'Eleanor?'

The woman barely blinked. She just turned her head and stared.

'Eleanor? It's me, Emma. Emma Jane Morgan.'

Emma watched as something registered in the woman's face and an unusual expression seemed to move across her eyes.

'Do you recognise me, Eleanor?'

But Eleanor didn't even open her mouth, she just shook her head and looked away.

Hurt, Emma stepped backwards until she walked right into Theodore.

'Oh, sorry.'

Both he and Declan looked down at her with sadness in their eyes.

'I know you really wanted to talk to her, mate. I'm sorry. Maybe she'll come round soon?' he said, trying to make her feel better.

'Yeah maybe,' Emma whispered. 'Thanks for letting me try. I've, er, got to go. I'll see you later,' she said absent-mindedly as she saw Diarmuid wave at her through the window in the door.

'Of course. You sure you're okay?' asked Declan as he stepped to one side to let her through.

'Yeah, yeah, I'm fine, thanks.'

Pushing open the door, Emma rushed out and grabbed Diarmuid's hand.

'Hey, how is she?' he asked, smiling. But when he saw the look on her face, he immediately stopped and pulled her towards him.

'Oh babe, what's up? What happened?'

Tears rolled down her cheeks as Emma let him hug her tightly, her arms circling his solid waist.

'Can we just go?' she asked, looking up into his eyes. 'I just need to get out of here.'

'Of course,' he said, picking up that there was something very wrong.

'Where do you want to go?' he whispered, giving her a stronger hug for a second before releasing his hold and pulling her away from the infirmary.

'Let's just go,' she said, allowing herself to be pulled.

'It's cold out there,' he said as she led them to the main exit door. 'Come on, let's grab our coats first.'

❦ 16 ❦

'I'm telling you something's seriously wrong,' Emma whispered as they pounded the pavements outside of Praxos Academy. 'We need to find Lana and Barber.'

'Oh, okay,' Diarmuid said. 'I left my phone charging in my room.'

'I have mine, but if they're on the motorbike, they might not hear it,' she said, as she pulled her mobile phone out of her pocket and dialled Lana's number.

Luckily, it rang for just a second before her sister picked up.

'Hey, Sis, what's up?'

'I need to talk to you. Where are you?' Emma said.

Immediately realising that something wasn't right, Lana gave her sister her full attention, 'We're not far away. We just stopped coz I needed a quick coffee before...'

'Yeah whatever, we just need to talk. We'll come to you. Which coffee shop are you in?'

'Starbucks.'

'We'll be there in ten minutes.'

Emma shoved the phone back in her pocket and linked arms with Diarmuid. 'We're going to Starbucks. Walk fast,' she instructed.

'You know, you've become far bossier since coming back from Canada,' he grinned, trying to lighten the mood.

But Emma's mood couldn't be lightened and so he quietened down and walked, wondering what on earth was going on. He knew though, that when she was so deep in thought, she shouldn't be interrupted.

About seven minutes later, they arrived at the nearest Starbucks. Pushing open the door, Emma was relieved to find it super busy. Lots of noise to make it easier to talk, she thought.

Scouring the tables, she soon spotted Lana waving frantically from the one table that was slightly around the corner, hidden somewhat from the rest of the clientele.

'Hey,' Lana said. 'You look like you could do with a hot drink. Barber, would you mind?'

Barber went to stand up.

'No, let me. I'll do it,' Diarmuid said with a smile.

'Green tea?' he asked, but she shook her head. 'No, not today. Today I think I need... I need... coffee.'

Lana gasped, 'But you never have coffee.'

Diarmuid and Lana shared a look, 'Coffee it is,' he said, walking away but suddenly stopping and turning. 'Barber, anything?'

Barber gave him an odd look and shook his head, before Diarmuid grinned for a second. 'Oh you're a vamp...er, sorry, forgot for a second.'

Ten minutes later, the four of them were sitting around the little table, Lana holding firmly onto Barber's hand, while in the other, she held a cup of now lukewarm hot mocha waiting to see what was so wrong. Emma had downed her Americano - much to the shock of the others - and was sitting quietly, trying to sort out the thoughts in her mind before she spoke.

'Babe?' Diarmuid asked. 'What's going on in there?'

Taking a deep breath, Emma looked into the eyes of each of her friends and sister.

'It's Eleanor.'

'Yeah, that much I gathered,' Lana breathed out.

Emma gave her a slightly unamused look before continuing.

'When I got to the infirmary, Theodore and Declan were there. Apparently she has lost her memory. She doesn't even know him, Declan or Wilbur.'

The others gasped.

'She doesn't know who anyone is. The best neurologists have already been to see her and they're baffled too.'

'Well, she has been through hell and back,' Diarmuid added. 'Memory loss can be triggered by all kinds of trauma.

'Yes I agree, it can,' Emma replied before she looked down at the table. 'But there's something else.'

'What Emma?' asked Barber who normally kept relatively quiet. 'What is it?'

'I wanted to see for myself so I spoke to her but she didn't know me either.'

'She wouldn't, if she doesn't know anyone else, why would she know you?'

'Yeah I know, but I just wanted to see her for myself, you know.'

Diarmuid put his hand over Emma's and she turned to look at him.

'This isn't the main reason I needed to talk to you.'

'There's more?' asked Lana.

Nodding, Emma sighed deeply, 'I don't think that's Eleanor in that hospital bed.'

Now the gasps were even more audible.

'What makes you say that?' asked Barber, concern written all over his face.

'The first inkling I got was when we pulled her from the tree. When I first healed her, there was something wrong, something odd about the place she'd been stabbed. Remember when Madge stabbed her before jumping into the wormhole?'

The others nodded.

'She ought to have some serious scar tissue beneath her skin. But there was nothing there.'

'Not even a scar?' asked Lana.

'A very faint scar, yes, but no scar tissue.'

'Maybe she was healed by a witch or something?'

'Yes that's possible I suppose but I don't think so.'

'Yes, why would Madge stab her and then heal her?' asked Barber, looking around at the others.

'When I said her name and she turned to look at me, I saw something else. It wasn't Eleanor. Eleanor would never look at me like that. It was evil. She tried to hide it, but I saw it first. I'm telling you, that woman in there is not Eleanor Hayden-Jones.'

'What do you propose we do about it?' asked Diarmuid. 'Shouldn't we tell Declan?'

Emma nodded, 'Yes, but I couldn't risk her hearing me in the infirmary. We need to get him out of the Academy.'

Suddenly Lana gasped.

'What?' Barber asked.

'John?' she murmured. 'What if John isn't really John too?'

Emma's eyes opened wide. 'Aria is with him. What if she's in danger as well?'

'I'll call Declan,' Barber said, dialling him on his outdated mobile phone.

'You really need a new phone, hon,' Lana commented as he put it to his ear.

'This is ok. I've had it years. It works.'

'To make phone calls. You can't do a single other thing with it,' she smiled.

'And why would I need to?' he half-joked before he saw Emma's serious face and they both dropped the conversation.

'Dec, we need you. Serious stuff. Yeah, uh huh? Yeah? Okay, the nearest Starbucks. We'll wait for you.'

'Is he coming straight away?' asked Emma.

Barber nodded. 'He knew something was up. He's very astute, Declan is.'

'You can say that again,' Emma replied, tapping her short fingernails on the table.

'Well, may as well have another drink while we're waiting,' Lana said, standing. 'I'll get them this time. Emma? Tea this time? Juice? Water?'

But Emma shook her head, 'Can I try the mocha coffee?'

'OMG I never thought I'd see the day. You're gonna be running around like a headless chicken after all this caffeine,' Lana said, before she asked Diarmuid what he wanted.

Twenty minutes later, the four of them were joined by Declan. The moment he stepped into the room, his face changed as he saw their expressions.

'Hey,' he said, 'Why didn't you speak to me back at Praxos?' he asked Emma after she'd explained him her theory.

'I couldn't risk her hearing, just in case I'm right, and that woman in there, isn't who she wants us to think she is.'

Declan nodded, his face looking thunderous.

'I can't believe it,' he whispered, his head in his hands. 'If you're right, Emma, that means Eleanor is still out there somewhere.'

'Oh My God, I never even considered that,' Lana cried, her hands covering her mouth, while Barber gingerly stroked her back.

'She might not have made it, after all,' Emma whispered.

'Let's not think about that right now, folks. Let's think about how we're going to reveal her true identity and find out why she is pretending to be our Guardian,' Declan urged.

'But how?' Diarmuid asked. 'And who do you think it is?'

'If anyone, it's got to be Madge, right?' Lana cried. 'Infiltrated Praxos for the second time.'

'Shhh we don't know that for sure,' Barber tried to reassure them all.

'We need to warn to everyone,' Emma faced Declan. 'Everyone in Praxos right now is is danger. What are we going to do?'

'Firstly, we need to stay calm,' Declan said. 'Secondly, we cannot reveal that we know. We must continue this pretence with her. The second she realises that we know the truth, all hell could break loose and that's the last thing we want.'

'But about John? We need to discover if he actually is John? Oh my God, what about that Skull we rescued? He's probably in on it as well. Where is he? Emma said, her voice quivering slightly.

'Don't worry about him, Emma. He's under lock and key somewhere safe, Declan whispered, 'John, on the other hand, was released from the hospital two days ago'.

❧ 17 ❧

'I still can't believe that it's really you,' Aria whispered as she laid in the arms of the man she'd loved for over a decade. The two of them were curled up on the sofa in Aria's rented house.

'I know, it's been a long time baby,' John replied, as he took another large swig of red wine.

'Are you sure you're okay to mix alcohol with your medication?' she asked, sitting up and stretching her arms up high.

'I'm not taking the meds,' he answered, before knocking back the remainder of the drink and putting the glass on the side table.

'But John, you need to take it. You've been through such a lot of trauma, both physical and mental. Your medication will help you get through this.'

'I don't need that shit,' he said.

'John, you never used to talk like that,' she said, looking at him sadly.

'Like you said, I've been through a lot of mental and physical trauma.'

Aria's features softened and she relaxed. 'Sorry, it's just so good to have you back. I can't take you for granted, I need to know you're going to be alright.'

'I'm going to be just fine. Now stop fussing. Come here,' he said, pulling her close to him and kissing her hard on the lips.

'John,' she murmured. 'We can't. You need to recover fully before we, you know, do anything, that might hurt you,' she smiled, pulling away.

But John pulled her even closer, kissing her until she had some difficulty breathing.

'J...J...o....' she squirmed beneath him. 'Stop,' she managed to shout, pushing him away and jumping up off the sofa. 'You're not the same,' she said, shaking. 'You've changed. You were always so gentle before.'

'Yeah, that was before,' he said, wiping his mouth roughly and sitting up. 'What time is it?'

Aria glanced at the clock on the mantelpiece, 'Just after four. Why? Are you hungry? Can I get you something to eat?'

'Yeah that would be good,' he grinned. 'Get me some food will ya?'

Aria winced at his words, not wanting to believe how this man had changed so much after being held in captivity for so long. She knew he would be different, but never thought in a million years that he could ever become aggressive and yet here he was, the epitome of John's true opposite.

'What would you like, John? I could make something or I could get a take out, perhaps?'

'Steak, rare,' he muttered, as he picked up the bottle of wine and filled his glass for the third time.

'But... but...you're a vegetarian?'

'Stopped being a vegetarian when they took me, Aria,' he smiled, his eyes twinkling with something she'd not noticed before.

Gasping, she took a step backwards, stumbling over her favourite Tibetan rug. Just about gaining her balance, she took a deep breath and turned away from him.

'Yes, yes of course. I'm sorry. I'll get you a steak, right away. What would you like with it? Mashed potatoes, with cream, just the way you you used to love it. Your favourite right?'

'Yeah, baby, that would be perfect. Rare steak with mashed potatoes made with full fat cream, just the way I used to love it. You're the best baby.'

Aria faked a smile and walked out of the room.

There was no way this was her John. He was a vegetarian and more importantly, he was allergic to cream.

The sound of her phone ringing made her stop in her tracks and she looked around for her handbag. Remembering she'd left it in the kitchen, she immediately rushed in and picked it up. It was Declan.

'Declan?' she whispered, closing the door behind her.

'It's not John,' she whispered to him, trying to hold the phone as close to her mouth as possible.

'I don't know who that is, but it's not my John.'

'Mate, calm down. That's why I'm ringing. We figured it out too. It's not Eleanor either. Can you get away from him safely?'

Tears began to slide down Aria's face and she nodded, knowing Declan couldn't actually see her.

'Where are you?' he asked. 'Are you at home?'

'Yes,' she whispered. 'Get out. Get out now. Make some excuse and go. Can you do that, Aria?'

She nodded, 'Yes, yes I can,' she replied, straightening herself up and wiping her eyes.

'Barber is already on his way. He should be there in no time. You have his number? Keep your phone close.'

Aria took a deep breath and pressed the off button.

She carefully put the phone back in her bag and straightened up.

'Honey,' she yelled through the door as she opened it. 'I'll need to go and get some steak, okay? I'll be back before you know it.'

John, or whoever he really was, stood on the other side and she shrieked loudly.

'Hey, what's got your goat?'

'Huh?' Aria asked, looking at him, trying to do her best to act normally.

'Oh John you made me jump. I wasn't expecting you to be standing right there on the other side of the door. I'm fine.'

But John shook his head, 'No, no. I don't think you are. Something's up and I intend to get to the bottom of it.'

Aria tried to take a step backwards but the fridge was in the way.

John smiled, slowly taking her handbag from her shoulder. She just stood there, ready to make her move. As he turned his attention briefly away from her, Aria kneed him hard in his groin, making him double over in pain.

'You witch,' he bellowed.

Before she was able to get away, he grabbed her from behind and pulled her down to the floor where he pinned her down.

Knowing flailing around would be useless, Aria just lay still, looking deep into the man's eyes.

'Who are you?' she asked. 'I know you're not really John. What have you done with him? Where is he?'

But the impostor merely laughed and tightened his grip on her wrists.

'We could have had some good times together, me and you. I was so close to getting my way with you, wasn't I? You almost fell for it. What gave me away? Am I too different from lover boy? Hey Aria? Don't you fancy me then?' he asked, laughing evilly.

But Aria just shook her head, 'You're nothing like John,' she spat. 'John is a real man. A gentle soul. Nothing like you. Show yourself. Show me the real you, you impostor.'

His eyes glowed in the darkening room but he wasn't ready to reveal himself just yet so instead, he glanced around and grabbed the nearest item, a saucepan.

Aria turned from looking at his face to the saucepan and quickly realised his intention. Before she had time to react, the saucepan came crashing down onto the side of her head.

❦ 18 ❦

When Barber arrived at the address Aria had given to Declan, he literally broke down the door. But once inside, he could see signs of a struggle but no sign of either Aria or the impostor pretending to be John. He searched the rooms for any evidence as to where he might've taken her but there was nothing. Returning outdoors, he scoured up and down the street trying to locate them but it was useless. Aria was gone.

Soon, Declan and the others arrived, hoping that either Emma or Lana might be able to work out where he'd taken her. Walking around the small house, neither sister could feel anything. After thirty minutes, they gave up, knowing that if either of them were going to have a vision, it would have already happened.

'What do we do now?'asked Diarmuid as they stood near the doorway.

'We must concentrate on Eleanor now,' Declan replied. 'Let's get back to the Academy and see if we can get through to that... woman.'

'But how?' asked Lana. 'We can't risk her finding out we know the truth otherwise she might kill Eleanor.'

'I know, but what else do we have to go on?'

'We have to reach out to the angel again, Sis,' Emma whispered. She was perched on the edge of the sofa, listening to the conversation as the others hovered by the door. 'He's the only one that can help us.'

'You mean she, right?' Lana replied.

Emma shrugged, 'Whatever,' as Lana nodded.

'You're right though.'

'Let's get back and you can try and get through to the angel there. Maybe some of the others can help you? In the meantime, I'll get hold of Giovanni and let him know what's going on,' said Declan.

'What about Marlene?' asked Emma. 'She needs to know the truth.'

'I know,' Declan replied. 'I'll find her when we get back. Come on, let's get out of here.'

'I'll go out the back door and make sure it's all locked up,' Emma said as the others went to go out the front entrance.

'I'll come with you,' said Diarmuid, following her through the kitchen until they reached the door which was still unlocked.

'Is the key there?' she asked, as they looked around for any sign of it.

'It's in the door,' he grinned, taking it out and handing it to her.

'Can't see the woods for the trees,' she smiled before her face dropped, remembering the trees containing all the dead bodies in Nova Scotia.

'Hey,' Diarmuid, whispered. 'You okay?'

'Just thinking what a stupid thing it was to say.'

'About the trees?' he asked. She nodded. 'Hey, don't beat yourself up. We'll get to the bottom of this.'

'I just have this horrible feeling we're too late. It's been weeks now. How could she survive?'

'Are you forgetting who she is, Em? She's the Guardian of the Fourth House of Praxos. She's been immortal for hundreds and hundreds of years - longer actually - and she's the strongest woman I've ever known. Not counting you, of course,' he said, pulling her towards him and holding her tight.

'Thanks, babe,' she whispered.

'Now come on, they're waiting for us out front.'

Emma opened the back door and put the key in the lock. She made sure it was firmly locked before they turned to walk down the couple of steps and out through the back garden. When they reached the little gate, something caught her eye on the top of the fence.

'Is that... blood?' she asked, getting close enough to touch it. As she did so, an intense pain seemed to hit her on the side of her head. Turning to look at Diarmuid, she placed her hand on her head before falling to the ground.

'Hey guys,' yelled Diarmuid as loud as he could, as he bent down to carefully pick up his girlfriend.

Declan and the others came running from round the corner while he held her in his arms.

'She spotted blood and then seemed to collapse. Is she having a vision, Lana?' he asked, concern written all over his face.

Lana leaned forward and looked at Emma's closed eyes. Her eyelids were fluttering rapidly. Lana nodded. 'Definitely.'

'We should get her inside,' Diarmuid said as he turned to go back up the steps.

'No, we need to get back to Praxos. Barber will carry her.'

Diarmuid wasn't so keen to hand over his precious cargo but he reluctantly did when he saw Barber's eyes.

'Don't worry, it'll be much easier for me to carry her than you, Diarmuid. She'll be fine.'

He nodded and let Barber take Emma from his arms while Lana patted him on the back.

'She'll be okay. She's in the best possible hands,' she smiled. 'Now let's go,' she urged as they all started moving quickly back towards the Academy.

'The sooner we get there, the better,' Declan said as they began a slow jog, careful not to draw too much attention to themselves.

oOo

EMMA'S HEAD WAS POUNDING AS SHE OPENED HER EYES AND found herself in semi-darkness. A faint stench of sewage seemed to fill the air. Where the heck was she?

As her eyes began to adjust to the lack of light, she looked around and found herself chained to something.

'This is weird,' she whispered. If this is a vision why am I chained up?'

Looking down at herself, she gasped at the sight of something she wouldn't normally see on herself. She was wearing beige heels and beige skinny jeans. And when she looked at her hands, she soon realised they weren't her own hands she was looking at. A pretty and familiar eternity diamond ring adorned her ring finger.

'Aria,' she whispered. 'I'm having a vision from Aria's point of view. Where am I?' she asked herself, searching around to get some sort of clue that would help them find the missing woman.

But all that she could ascertain was that they were somewhere near sewage - the stench was getting stronger.

Screwing up her nose, she pulled on the chain, trying to loosen it's hold on her but it was a struggle, there was no way she could release herself.

Taking short breaths so she didn't have to breathe in too much of that awful smell, she continued to wiggle it, hoping that she might somehow loosen it, but it was no good. Instead, she soon realised the chain was attached to a long pipe so she could at least move a little.

Standing up, she began to take baby steps, feeling along the wall to try and find a clue.

Was she in a tunnel? Emma thought. Like the tunnels leading in and out of Praxos, the ones they used to use all the time when they'd first arrived at Praxos? Yes, Emma thought. It's definitely tunnel-like. She tried to remember all the places she'd been to over the past couple of years but none of them had that awful stench.

But that was a good thing. Once she got back from the vision, this would help them narrow it down. What else? What else could she see?

Stumbling over something on the ground, Emma stopped and crouched down. It was darker down this part of the tunnel and more difficult to see so she stretched out her hands as much as possible considering the chain restraints.

Gasping, she yanked her hands back before remembering she could easily create her own light. Cursing under her breath, she began to focus all her energy on the light source from within but after a few minutes of nothing, Emma swore loudly.

While having the vision via Aria's perspective, there was no way she could use her own powers. She would have to identify whatever was on the ground using touch, so she took a deep breath, almost choking as the smell travelled down into her lungs. Coughing, she stood back up for a second, her hands covering her mouth, before holding her breath and crouching back down.

She soon became all too aware at what was at her feet. It was a body. Someone else had been chained up and left for dead. But was he or she dead? And who was it?

Emma nearly choked. Leaning back against the wall, she looked upwards for a second, trying to get some air into her lungs that wasn't full of that foul smell.

Trying to take a deeper breath before she returned her attention to the body on the ground, Emma leaned forward and moved her hands across the person until she stopped at their wrist. Lifting the arm, she closed her eyes and waited, hoping to find some semblance of life. Some tiny movement. But she could feel nothing. So she leaned forward and very carefully put her head on their chest, hoping that there would at least be a heartbeat, even if it was a faint one. But she couldn't gauge anything. The person was wearing a thick leather jacket over a thick jumper. So she tried something else, feeling around until she found the person's face.

As she let her hands tell her who it was, Emma realised it was a man, a very thin man with quite a lot of facial hair. Leaning as far forward as the chain would allow her, she tilted the man's head back slightly before putting her ear over the man's mouth. It was almost too faint to feel, but she caught it. The faintest of breaths. Whoever he was, he was still alive, barely.

Immediately, Emma remembered everything she'd learned in class. But a familiar sensation began to come over her and so she very quickly rolled him over onto to his side and put him, as best she could, into recovery position before she leaned back against the wall and waited for the vision to end.

Opening her eyes, she found herself being carried through the streets of London.

'Huh?' she mumbled. 'What's going on?'

'It's okay, Emma. We're on our way back to Praxos,' Barber said as they rushed forward.

Turning to look to her side, she noticed Declan, Diarmuid and Lana all running alongside them.

'You okay, Sis?' Lana asked when she realised she'd come to.

Emma nodded but said nothing.

'I'll hold on to you until we get there,' Barber smiled, 'Just in case you're feeling a bit woozy.'

'Thanks Barber,' she smiled.

'Hey,' Diarmuid mouthed as she looked across at him, jogging by her side. 'You okay?'

She nodded and smiled at him before she let her head rest back on Barber's chest, knowing she would have been in no fit state to run across London after the vision she'd just had.

❦ 19 ❦

Eleanor's impostor was still laid up in the Praxos infirmary, acting as if she'd lost her memory. The majority of the students and even some of the teachers had not been told the truth, in order to maintain a cloak of secrecy. Declan didn't want to risk the impostor figuring out they knew the truth, so he kept his visits to a minimum, allowing only a few nurses to attend to her. However, he did make sure that there was always a certain number of Watchers covertly guarding the infirmary, keeping him well informed of everything that was happening down there.

In the meantime, he and those that knew the truth were busy trying to find Aria - made a little easier thanks to Emma's unusual vision. They now knew which tunnels to dismiss from their search.

Since the vision, both Emma and Lana had tried to return to it, but to no avail. It was almost as if something was preventing their visions from happening as often as they used to.

Even their attempts to contact the angel had been without result.

'It's so frustrating,' Lana had cried, throwing herself onto her bed. 'We're getting nowhere and nothing seems to be helping. It's like someone up there,' she pointed skywards, 'is trying to stop us from discovering the truth, not the other way round. I thought he said he - she - was going to help us? I'm so confused.'

'I know. Me too,' sighed Emma from the other side of the room where she sat brushing her hair. 'It's almost like there's some kind of blockage.'

'Yeah, that's exactly what it's like,' Lana replied, sitting upright. 'What if that's exactly it?' she suddenly asked.

'What? That someone is blocking us?'

'Exactly.'

'But who would do that? And why?'

'The Skulls maybe?' Lana pondered.

'The Skulls are always responsible.'

'Usually, yes,' Lana said as she kicked off her knee high boots and replaced them with her favourite pair of sheepskin ones.

'But what if we're supposed to be working this out? Maybe it's a test?'

Emma stopped brushing her hair and turned to look at her sister, 'A test? Really? Eleanor being stabbed and kidnapped and returned as an impostor, with John, and blocking us from achieving our true powers and you think it's a test? Come on, Lana. Get real.'

Lana looked down, a little embarrassed. 'Yeah, sorry. I'm just so confused with all this. It makes me want to scream. I wanna know what's really going on. I mean, where is the real Eleanor? And John? And why can't we communicate with her anymore? I just want life to go back to the way it was before all of this. Back to the beginning.'

'Yeah, you and me both, Lana.'

Emma returned her attention to the mirror and put the brush down before slowly turning back to look at her sister. 'Actually, I wonder if there's something in that,' she wondered.

'What do you mean?'

'Back to the beginning. Back to where this all started.'

'What, you mean us coming to Praxos?'

Emma's lips twisted sideways as she thought for a minute.

'No, back to the beginning of this whole thing with Madge here at Praxos.'

'You mean Sthenelaus?'

Emma winced very slightly and shook her head, 'No, the swimming pool.'

'Oh right,' Lana said as if she knew what Emma was talking about. 'Actually no. No idea what you mean.'

'We were in the pool having fun, when all this began, right? Maybe we need to get back into the same pool and see what happens?'

'Oh, er, okay? If you really think that will help?'

'I really have no idea if it will help but... it did just come to me and I have this feeling...'

'Ooh one of your gut feelings?'

Emma nodded.

'Then what are we waiting for. Let's go. Shall we tell the others?'

Emma shook her head, 'They're all busy investigating other possibilities. Let's do this alone. Just you and me, like in the old days.'

'The old days?' Lana grinned. 'I like the way that you put that. Not that the old days was that long ago,' she chuckled.

'Well, you know what I mean. You ready for this?'

Lana jumped up and scrambled into her wardrobe.

'What are you looking for?' asked Emma as she stood up, ready to go.

'This,' she pulled out her swimming costume before rushing to Emma's much smaller wardrobe and rummaged around until she found her sister's too.

'I was just gonna go in like this,' Emma said, looking down at her jeans and long sleeved t-shirt.

'Really? You'll be far more comfortable actually dressed for the pool. Plus, it'll help you relax and well, you know, that just might help us somehow.'

'I guess so,' Emma said as she took the swimsuit off her sister and they went to rush out of the room.

'Oh hang on a sec,' Emma said, turning back. 'I have an idea.'

'Huh?' Lana replied.

'This belonged to Eleanor. You never know, it might help.'

Lana looked confused.

'When we used the Praxos pool before we managed to have a vision about Madge using that watch Sthenelaus gave to Aria'

'Don't remind me,' Lana muttered, 'That was what really started it. That bloody woman had been using it to listen in to everything.'

The girls walked through the corridor until they reached the great hall before going down one of the darker tunnels, past the archives until they stood in front of a large oval wooden door. The girls glanced at each other, made sure no-one was around to see them, before they pushed the door open and walked inside,

revealing a room that looked like something from an aquarium. Directly in front and above was a massive glass pool, illuminated from beneath.

'Even though we had a hell of a dodgy experience in here the last time, it's still pretty cool,' Lana smiled as they quickly got changed in the changing room, grabbing a towel each before they climbed the steps towards the far end of the pool.

'Yes it is,' Emma smiled. 'I won't let Madge spoil it for me.'

Before Lana could respond, Emma had dived into the deep end, leaving her sister to slowly lower herself in.

'I'm glad they kept the pool heated,' she muttered to herself as she immersed herself completely into the water, leaving just her head above it. Locating Emma beneath and taking a deep breath, Lana swam to the bottom of the pool.

Emma opened her eyes the second her sister arrived and, together, they locked hands, keeping the trinket that belonged to Eleanor tightly within their palms. Lana opened her eyes then, and waited for Emma to create a bubble so she could breathe. Smiling as the small bubble began to increase in size until it enveloped them both, allowing them both to breathe freely, Lana smiled.

'You ready?'

Emma nodded, 'You?'

The second Lana nodded, both girls closed their eyes and waited, focussing on the object between their fingers.

It didn't take long for Emma's initial gut feeling to pay off.

After feeling like they'd been through a washing machine, tumbling around and around, both girls opened their eyes.

'Oh, I feel so sick,' Lana coughed as they washed up on the shore of a familiar beach.

'We're back in Canada. Oh My God, we're back in Canada,' Emma repeated. 'Are you alright? she asked as Lana stood up, pulling her up at the same time.

'Yeah, just a bit nauseous. That was a first. It was horrible.'

'Yeah, maybe because we crossed continents or something,' Emma suggested.

'I wonder why it brought us back to the beach though?'

Emma shrugged and followed Lana as they climbed over bits of driftwood and rocks until they eventually stood at the foot of the forest where they'd previously found all those dead bodies hidden in the trees.

Lana shivered.

'You cold?' Emma asked.

'It's not really that,' Lana sighed, looking up at the vegetation.

'Yeah I know what you mean. But we need to figure this out before the vision fades. You ready?'

'Bring it on,' Lana smiled.

Climbing over a few more larger rocks, they rushed through the trees, heading towards the old wooden house.

'Wait,' Lana suddenly shouted. 'Over there, look,' she pointed towards the other more impressive house where someone appeared at the door.

'Follow him,' Emma instructed.

Running as fast as they could, the sisters soon found themselves standing behind a young man dressed rather oddly.

'He looks like he belongs on a historical film set,' Lana whispered.

'Why are you whispering, Sis? He can't hear us.'

'Oh yeah, I always forget about that. Where's he going?'

'I dunno. Let's just follow him and see,' Emma said as they moved directly behind him, following as he walked through the large kitchen and down some steps until he reached a heavy wooden door. Taking a large key out of his pocket, he unlocked it and walked in.

On the other side was another massive iron door.

'I don't remember seeing any of this. Do you?'

Emma shook her head. 'There were no steps and no door when we came. They must've blocked them off somehow.'

Suddenly, both girls dropped to the floor, their hand covering their ears as an intense high pitched howling sound pierced the air around them.

'What is that? What's happening?' Lana shrieked. 'It hurts so bad.'

But as soon as it had begun, it came to a halt and the girls were able to release the hold over their ears.

'What was that?' Emma cried.

'Maybe that's the sound that blocked Declan? God, is that what he was going through that whole time we were here? That must've been horrendous. But what the heck was it? And why couldn't we hear it before.'

Both girls shrugged and turned their attention back to the odd looking young man who had now opened the iron door.

'It was him, it must have been. The door must have some kind of spell on it - some kind of curse maybe?' Emma suggested.

'Maybe,' Lana agreed. 'I'm just glad it's over. What's behind the door?'

'I can't see.'

Just as the girls tried to follow the man inside, that all too familiar sensation began to creep into their bones.

'No, not now,' screamed Emma. 'No!'

But it was no good, the vision was ending, they were returning to the Praxos swimming pool. At least they thought they were returning to the Praxos swimming pool.

❧ 20 ☙

Opening her eyes, Emma sat up quickly and scoured the area around her. She noticed Lana was laying on the floor to her side.

'Lana, wake up,' she said, roughly shoving her sister. 'Wake up,' she urged.

Lana groaned and rolled over, 'What happened?'

'We're not in Kansas anymore Toto,' Emma whispered.

'Oh no, we're not. Where are we?' Lana whispered as she sat up and they both peered around them. They soon realised not only were they not at the house in Nova Scotia, but they also were no longer in the Praxos swimming pool either.

'I don't know,' Emma whispered.

'You're somewhere completely different,' said a familiar voice from above them.

'You again,' said Lana, looking up. 'We've been trying to reach you. We needed your help and you wouldn't come.'

'I am sorry,' said the voice. 'Sometimes it's just not impossible to get through to you. I have tried to, I assure you I have.'

The man's voice began to fade a little.

'Wait,' Emma cried, standing up. 'Please don't go. Why did you bring us here now? And where are we? And, who are you? Truly?'

Lana was now standing beside Emma in a vast open plain.

Nothing but thick white clouds surrounded them. Both stood with their heads tilted back as they stared into nothingness.

'Where are you? We can't see you?' Lana shouted. 'Show yourself.'

Their surroundings began to morph into something else and then they found themselves standing on a mountaintop. The clouds drifted from all around them, moving upwards and then a dark-skinned man appeared in the distance walking towards them, like a mirage in a desert.

'It is me and you are currently standing on a mountain in the Himalayas,' he chuckled. 'Beautiful isn't it?'

'But who is me? I mean you? Oh you know what I mean,' Lana stuttered, embarrassed.

'I'm sorry you have not felt like I have been helping you, but I cannot always do that. I am prevented from doing so. In fact, sometimes we are all prevented from doing so.'

'You're like some kind of cryptic crossword,' Lana shivered. 'You're just confusing the hell out of me,' she cried, stamping her feet.

'Please refrain from using that word. They don't like it so much,' said the man.

'Who doesn't like it?' asked Emma.

The man looked upwards.

'But you're one of them so why does it matter?' said Lana.

'I am not one of them, not yet. I haven't been one of them for quite some time, but almost. I'm almost there. Soon, soon I will be home.'

'Home? Why do you always talk in riddles? We don't have a clue what you're talking about. We just want your help to find Eleanor and John and to finally put Madge behind bars,' Emma cried, shivering slightly.

'Oh forgive me, girls. You must be quite chilly up here.'

Suddenly, their surroundings changed. The mountains disappeared, to be replaced by the most beautiful exotic beach. Dolphins majestically jumped in and out of the ocean in front of them, while palm trees swayed in the warm breeze behind them. Their feet sank into the wet sand as the shoreline moved with the tide. Meanwhile, the sun shone down upon them, warming their swimsuit clad bodies.

'Better?' he asked.

Both girls reluctantly nodded before Lana added, 'So, are you going to tell us who you are? And why did you pull us out of our vision like that? We were so close to finding out the truth.'

'The truth?' he asked as he walked towards the water, his white cloak trailing in the ocean.

The girls both nodded.

'I'm not sure you're quite ready for the truth.'

'Of course we are,' Emma responded quickly. 'We can't move on with our lives until we do. And you're the one that told us that we need to fight and to move on and live our lives.'

The man smiled, 'So you were listening?'

'Of course.'

'But the truth is painful, Emma, Lana. Are you ready for that kind of pain?'

'We're ready to become our true selves. We are Watchers. Eleanor taught us that. Yes we're ready,' Lana said confidently.

Emma looked at her sister and smiled. She took her hand in her own and squeezed it.

The man stood looking at them. He nodded.

'Yes, I believe you are.'

Within a matter of seconds, the man was no longer standing beside them; the ocean, palm trees and sun had disappeared.

They were back in Nova Scotia, standing where the odd young man had been standing before. The iron door was wide open. Holding on to each other's hands, the sisters walked forward and tentatively walked down the steep steps they found in front of them.

It was quite dark, so they had to go slowly to allow their eyes to adjust.

'Are you ready for this?' Emma asked.

'I'm ready to get to the bottom of this. It's time,' she answered, looking somewhat fearful at what they might find.

Once they'd reached the last step, they turned a corner and walked along a narrow tunnel, leading to what appeared to be the very base of a tree, roots intertwined and spreading all around them.

Looking upwards, they gasped.

❦ 21 ❧

There, right in front of them and hanging in chains, was Eleanor.

'Oh My God, Eleanor,' cried Emma as she rushed forward trying to release the chains, but it was no good. This was nothing but a vision. Eleanor was in Canada. They were in London.

'Is she... is she... dead?' whispered Lana as she just stood there trying to look away from the woman who had changed their lives in such a positive way.

'I... I... I don't know,' whispered Emma. 'But what I do know is that we need to get out of this vision so we can alert Giovanni straight away.'

'Wait Emma. What about John? We need to see if he's here?'

'No, Giovanni can do that. We must tell him about this now.'

Lana nodded and so the sisters stood facing each other, holding hands, focussing on returning to Praxos. But nothing happened.

'What's going on?' Emma whispered. 'We need to get back.'

'I don't know. Something's stopping us. Try again.'

They closed their eyes, thinking of nothing but getting back home.

Nothing

'Oh My God, I can't believe this,' Lana whispered. 'Maybe we need to see more first. Maybe there's something else really important we need to discover?'

Emma opened her eyes and tears began to roll down her cheeks as she turned her attention back to Eleanor.

'Eleanor, Eleanor can you hear me? I'm so sorry, I'm sorry we couldn't find you in time. I'm sorry you had to endure this. It's not fair,' she fell to her knees and sobbed.

Suddenly, the girls realised they were no longer alone.

'Hello?' Lana whispered as she looked around. 'Who's there?'

Emma lifted her head. 'What's happening, Sis? Isn't it just that guy who opened the door?'

'No, it's someone who knows we're here. I can feel it.'

'It's just me,' said a voice from the shadows.

Stepping out of the darkness came the angel they'd spoken to earlier.

'You? Why are you here?' Lana asked, confused.

'Because I am not who I seem.'

Both girls stood up and watched as the man's features began to change, his skin colour faded from dark to light and his hair began to grow longer and blonde.

'We saw you change before, we just caught sight of your hair. We don't understand,' Emma stuttered.

When the transformation was complete, both girls stumbled backwards, holding on to each other for support.

'E...e...l...eanor?' they both whispered.

The woman nodded. 'I am so sorry, girls. I wanted to tell you, I wanted to spare you all of this. I truly did. But they would not allow me to communicate with you directly while I still... lived.'

'Lived?' Emma murmured, turning to look at the body hanging in chains.

'That's right, my dear Emma. I am no longer living. I am so sorry.'

Emma's knees buckled and she fell forward.

Lana steadied her.

'Why? You're immortal. Why now, after all this time? I don't understand? And why the man? Who was he? Why couldn't you show your true self?'

'Please don't cry, my dear Morgan sisters. You found me and now that you have found me, I can be at peace. You've given me that. Both of you have given me that and I will therefore be eternally grateful.'

'Why not before?' asked Lana.

'Girls, please understand that my human body has only just passed. Just moments ago. I could only use Tarquin's body as a vessel while I lived. And even then it was quite a feat.'

'Tarquin? Your husband?' Emma whispered, lifting her head and looking at this angelic Eleanor standing before them.

Eleanor beamed, 'Yes, I am finally able to be with him. After all these hundreds and hundreds of years. You see, I am now able to be happy, knowing that my daughter Marlene is finally where she should be, and I am finally where I should be. With Tarquin,' she smiled.

'You stalled us,' Lana slowly cried. You stopped us from finding you in time, didn't you?' she accused.

Eleanor turned to face the young woman and smiled sadly. 'It was my time. I've been waiting for so long, Lana. And when I found Tarquin, I knew I couldn't return. Please understand that it was my time.'

'But we could have saved you?' she sobbed. 'Emma could have saved your life.'

Eleanor moved a little closer, 'I have no doubt about that, sweet girls, but it was not what I wanted. It was not meant to happen that way. It was my time, that is all.'

'But you should be with us,' Emma cried, the tears rolling down her cheeks once more.

But Eleanor shook her head, 'I have always been with you and I always will be, in my own special way. I knew you would find me. And now you have given me peace.'

'But...but... Eleanor...'

'There are no buts now, my dear Lana. Now that I have passed, it is time for a new era at Praxos. Declan will take my place as Guardian of the Fourth House of Praxos and you, Emma, will work closely by his side with Diarmuid,' she smiled.

'I will?'

Eleanor nodded. 'Eventually, the role of Guardian will become yours, but only once Declan has completed his work. But this will not happen for many years to come.'

'But nothing is going to happen to Declan, right?' Lana sobbed.

'No, of course not. But eventually he will want to move with his children to another place.'

'His children?' asked Emma. 'But he doesn't have any?'

Again, Eleanor smiled. 'Saleena is already with child, but shhh-hhh, don't tell him I told you. He does not yet know.'

Lana and Emma grinned in between their tears.

'And you, my dearest Lana. You are the spark that makes Praxos special. You have a long and wonderful future ahead of you. And yes, before you ask, Barber just happens to be a part of that future, which is funny. I never thought you'd settle down with one man but he is a special soul, that vampire. There'll be lots of excitement and travel in your future,' she smiled.

Emma looked at her sister and smiled, 'I always knew that about her,' she whispered, looking back at Eleanor.

'Now, please don't mourn me. And tell all of my wonderful family at Praxos the truth. That I have finally found peace with Tarquin, it's what I always wanted. I am profoundly happy and profoundly grateful for having been a part of your lives, and for having been a Guardian of Praxos. I will continue to watch you all. Perhaps one day, I will see you again. Should you ever need my help, I will come. But I have a feeling that you will do just fine without me.'

'Please don't leave us, Eleanor. Please don't go. We're not ready for you to go,' Emma sobbed.

'Emma Jane Morgan, you are more ready now than ever. The same goes for you, Lana Beth Morgan. Take care of each other, live with laughter, live with love, live amazing lives. I will always love you both dearly, as if you were my own daughters. Just like Marlene...'

'Wait, what about Marlene?' Emma suddenly asked.

'She has grown into a wonderful, strong woman. It is time for her to live her life free of constraints. She can finally be a part of Praxos and I know she is going to make an amazing Guardian of the Fifth House of Praxos.'

'She's a Guardian too?' asked Lana.

Eleanor nodded, 'Soon. Now I must go and so must you. It is time for you to put my body to rest so that I can be entirely free.

John is still alive, you must find him and heal him quickly. Find him, my girls. Find him.'

Eleanor faded away.

'No, no, no, no, no.... don't go,' yelled Emma as she rushed forward to the place Eleanor's spirit had been gently hovering.

'She's gone, Emma. We have to respect her wishes now. She's happy, hon. Really happy. She finally got her man back. Let's not cry too much,' but Lana's voice cracked and she sniffed loudly.

'Easier said than done, right?' asked Emma as they hugged each other.

'Farewell, farewell,' whispered a voice in the shadows as the girls fell into a tumble, rolling around as if trapped in rough ocean waves, until eventually, they opened their eyes and found themselves back at the bottom of the Praxos pool.

❧ 22 ❧

Giovanni stood at the foot of the stairs, several soldiers standing beside him. Taking a deep breath, he nodded sideways. The small group backed away, hiding behind the solid kitchen island while Giovanni gave another nod to a fourth soldier by the door.

'Fire in the hole,' yelled the man.

They all crouched down and waited for the explosive device to break through the door. Following the blast, the soldiers rushed forward, pushing it open and, with guns in hand, investigated below.

Giovanni soon followed, preparing himself for the gruesome sight of the corpse of the woman he'd grown very fond of in recent months.

As expected, the stench of death filled his nostrils and he almost gagged. Covering his mouth and nose with his hand, he continued forward down the steps and along the dark corridor until he reached the tree roots the girls had told him about on the phone. And then a few more steps and he found himself standing in front of her. Eleanor.

'Get her down immediately,' he commanded. 'Carefully,' he added softly.

'Oh Eleanor,' he whispered tenderly once she was laid on the floor. 'I know you're long gone but travel well. I'll miss you. We all will. Be at peace with Tarquin now. You deserve that.'

Covering her face before wiping his eyes roughly, he instructed his guys to remove her body from the dark tunnel, ready to be transported back to London where she would finally be allowed to be laid to rest.

As her body was very carefully carried away, Giovanni took his time to investigate beneath the tree above, trying to find further clues as to where John might be, as well as to the whereabouts of the man both Emma and Lana had followed there.

But there was nothing. The area contained nothing but tree roots and Eleanor's corpse hanging in chains.

Punching the wall, Giovanni's eyes began to change colour while anger filled his every pore. Taking a moment to breathe deeply, he turned away, rushing through the darkness and up the steps, two at a time, bursting through the kitchen and out into the fresh air.

A deep growl erupted from his throat as his clothes ripped from his strong body and his limbs cracked as he made his transformation into a large angry werewolf. Once the change was complete, he let out a terrifying howl.

His soldiers watched him change before they all looked at each other, nodded, and hopped into the helicopter, closing the door behind them as Giovanni was left to roam the forest beyond.

Eventually lifting into the air, the chopper hovered for a few seconds before flying away into the distance.

Giovanni looked up at the sky and watched his men disappear before he returned his attention to the woods surrounding him. He would find the wretch that assisted in killing Eleanor if it was the last thing he did.

＊ 23 ＊

ria awoke with a start, momentarily forgetting where she
was. When the stench filled her nostrils, it all came
flooding back. John had attacked her. Only he wasn't John,
was he? It was someone else, an impostor, posing as John. She
sobbed loudly. Wiping her nose roughly, she realised she was still
chained up. The tunnel.

He'd dumped her here and she'd tried to walk the length of the
tunnel when she'd stumbled over something on the ground. It was
a body, a man's body. The memory, which was odd and somewhat
surreal, came back to her. She'd found a faint pulse and had turned
him on his side. Recovery position. Then she must have
passed out.

Feeling around in the semi-darkness, she'd found the man's
hands, both restrained with what felt like rope. She could just
about reach them. His hands were so cold and bony.

'Can you hear me?' she whispered. 'I know you're so close to
death but you must summon what strength you have left. You must
survive this,' she urged as she fumbled with the rope, trying everything she could to undo it. 'Whoever you are, you don't deserve
this.'

Her fingers eventually managed to undo the knot tying his
hands together and she breathed a sigh of relief as she gently

rubbed his wrists, moving her hands up and down, trying to warm his hands.

'This isn't doing any good,' she whispered. 'I wish I had the powers of Emma Jane. If she were here, she could heal you.' Sighing, she turned her attention to the man's face, gently bringing her fingers to his forehead. It was freezing cold.

She sat back, thinking hard, trying to focus on her own power as a Watcher. Trying to summon up the strength to make it work for her in the situation. But how could it? She was never particularly strong or fast. She wasn't able to read minds, or move things without touching them. She couldn't conjure up heat or fire. Healing wasn't something she'd ever been able to do. No, her strong points were her abilities to comfort people in need. Aria was a listener. There whenever the Watchers needed a shoulder to cry on.

She cursed herself under her breath. 'How is that going to help me now,' she seethed.

'You're such a strong woman. You're like Wonder Woman,' another distant memory floated in her mind. 'Aria, you've always been the girl for me. I wish we'd met when we were kids, so we could've had even more years together.'

John's words rang in her ears and she rested her head against the wall as she reminisced the little time they had shared.

'We're going to grow old together, you and me. I just know it,' he'd whispered as they'd laid together on the grass at the Greenwich Observatory looking up at the stars.

'John and Aria. Together forever,' Aria had replied with a smile, turning her face to watch him smile.

'Together forever,' she whispered now. 'John and Aria. Together forever,' she repeated louder, and again, louder and louder until she was shouting as loud as she could.

The man by her side made a faint groaning sound and she immediately turned towards him, getting up onto her knees so she could listen intently.

'Can you hear me?' she whispered.

Again, he groaned.

'You can?' she exclaimed, reaching out to touch his hands.

Taking them in hers, she very gently squeezed.

'Can you tell me who you are?'

But the man just groaned again, slightly louder this time.

'I'm sorry we're in this predicament, but my friends are looking for me. I'm sure of it. Please try and stay strong. I know it's tough, but you must.'

'I...I...'

'You?'

'W...a...t...e...r...' he managed to murmur.

'I'm sorry, I don't have any,' she cried. 'But... but the wall is very damp if we could lift you up, you could try and lick it,' she said, feeling like a total idiot for suggesting such a thing.

The man tried lifting his hands, but his body was altogether far too weak. It was impossible. He couldn't move, not at all.

'I'm sorry,' Aria whispered as she banged the back of her head against the wall, wincing when she remembered how that impostor had hit her with a saucepan.

What can I do, what can I do, she thought over and over again.

'Su.....' the man groaned.

'Su...what are you trying to say?' she asked, leaning over him and trying hard to listen.

He tried again, 'Sum...'

'Summer? Huh? I'm sorry, I don't know what you're trying to say.'

'Su...mm...on..'

'Summon? But summon what?' she asked eagerly.

'W...a...t...e...r.'

'I don't have any. I'm sorry,' but she suddenly remembered something. It was like a light switch going on in her head.

'Summon the water? Oh gosh, yes, why didn't I think of that. You're a genius!'

Hopping up onto her feet, she placed her hands onto the damp wall and remembered something her brother, Luis, had taught her when she younger. Luis had always been keen to learn survival techniques and, being a Watcher, had always got a thrill when specials powers came into it.

'You can do it, Sister. Just have faith in yourself. Remember you're a Watcher and we can do anything we put our minds to,' she recalled. They'd been playing outside the Praxos villa in the hills of

Monchique, trying to create wind, water and fire. How on earth could she have forgotten something so important. It was like a memory she'd erased from her consciousness. But why?

As the memory grew stronger, she soon realised why she'd forgotten it. She'd been so ashamed of herself that she'd pushed it back to the far recesses of her mind.

'I can do it, Luis. Let me do it,' she'd giggled, watching as the flames had danced in front of her. Flames that she'd created, purely through focus and concentration. Soon, she had created enough wind to move the fire back and forth in front of them.

'You did it, you did it,' Luis laughed, clapping his hands. 'Well done. Now you must extinguish them.'

But the fire had begun to move rapidly through the dry trees and bushes along the hills. Soon it was raging, billowing black clouds of smoke. She recalled how she'd been filled with dread and terror.

'Put it out, put it out,' Luis has screamed at her. But she couldn't do it. There was too much fear in her heart.

'I can't Luis, I can't do it. Please do it, please stop it from spreading,' but the water Luis had summoned hadn't been enough. The fire spread, causing widespread panic in the nearby town, people had to leave their homes while the fire brigade got to work. Fortunately, nobody had lost their lives but two houses had been destroyed.

Aria felt her face turn crimson red. She'd been responsible for that fire, had created it using her own powers as a Watcher, with her own two hands.

But that wasn't important now. What was important was that she'd been able to create fire and wind but could she create water? Could she?

'Su...mm...on... the water...' croaked the man.

Aria nodded and leaned forward, both hands flat against the wall. She cleared her mind of everything, trying not to remember all the awful things she'd witnessed over the last few months. Her mind had to be empty of all things, except the need for water.

'Focus,' she said to herself quietly. 'Water,' she whispered. 'Come to me now.'

She whispered the same words over and over again until she felt a gentle surge beneath her fingertips.

Opening her eyes, she felt a trickle of water fall onto the palm of her hand.

'It worked, it worked,' she yelled, giggling like the confident child she'd once been, before the Monchique fire had extinguished her true abilities as a Watcher.

'Wa...t...e...r,' croaked the man next to her.

'Yes, yes, of course. Sorry,' she said as she deftly let the palm of her hand fill up with the fresh water. Carefully carrying it down towards his mouth, she let him drink from her hand.

Initially, he coughed and spluttered it all over her, but now with a constant supply, she simply returned to the source and filled it up again until he'd had his fill.

'Thank you,' he managed to whisper. His throat no longer excruciatingly dry.

'My pleasure,' she smiled as she brushed her hand against his.

'You're so cold though,' she said. We need to get you warmed up.'

'F...ire?' he asked expectantly.

Could she? Could she conjure up a small fire to warm them up? After all this time, could she control it? Worried that she might produce too much and they'd be engulfed by flames, Aria sat down beside him.

'I... I don't know if I can do it,' she whispered, but the man murmured something to spur her on.

'You... can do... it. You're a strong... woman.'

'Yes, I guess so but...'

'You're... like... Won...der...'

Aria gasped, her hands covering her mouth. Was he going to say Wonder Woman?

'...W...o...man.'

'John,' she shrieked. 'Oh My God, is it really you this time? How could I not know? You're half the man you were. Jesus, what did that witch do to you?'

Leaning forward, she pulled the frail man towards her, trying to push his long hair away from his face. She wanted to see his face, but the darkness wasn't enough.

Fire, she thought. She needed to make fire. Not just for warmth, but also so she could finally see his face. His real face. After all this time.

'Ar...ia,' his voice broke. 'I...m...sor...ry.'

'For what? You have nothing to be sorry for. That awful family took you from me all those years ago. God knows what they put you through. I've tried so hard to find you, my love. And now, here we are, chained up in a tunnel beneath the city, left to die.'

'At... least... we...'re....toge...'

'Together?' Aria asked. 'Yes, we will always be together, John. Even if we die here, at least we're together now.'

'No...not die,' he murmured. 'Fire.'

With a sudden burst of energy, Aria realised she had to try. If she failed, he was right. At least they were together.

'Fire, John. I'm going to do it. I'm going to make fire.'

$$\approx \quad 24 \quad \approx$$

Giovanni had caught the scent of a human. It was an unusual scent, one he'd not picked up on before, therefore he knew it didn't belong to any of his men.

Following it, with his nose to the forest floor, he soon found himself at the edge of the ocean. Lifting his nose to the air, he sniffed, growling at the sight of a boat in the distance. That's where he would find him.

Running to the back of the wooden house, where his men had left him a car with supplies, he let out another deep howl before he allowed his form to return to that of a human. Standing completely naked in the cold, he opened the car door and pulled out a bag with several sets of clothing.

Once dressed, he made a quick phone call.

Soon afterwards, Giovanni watched from the beach as a number of vessels and a helicopter descended on the distant boat. He took a deep last inhalation of his cigarette and flicked the butt onto the ground, twisting his foot on top of it, pushing it deep into the sand.

His phone buzzed. Looking down, he read the three words he'd wanted to hear so badly.

'We got him.'

A dark smile etched across his face as he turned to walk back up the beach, through the woods until he reached his car. Climbing in, he raced away, eager to get face to face with one of the people responsible for Eleanor's death.

oOo

'No, Giovanni,' Declan said on the other end of the phone. 'We cannot, under any circumstances, hurt him. We need him to find Aria and John, the real John and he must know Madge's plan. We could do with knowing that too.'

Reluctantly, Giovanni agreed.

'And the impostor in the hospital?' he asked. 'What of her?'

'She's still in there, and as far as she's concerned, we are all completely unaware of the truth. I want to keep it that way. At least until we find John and Aria.'

Giovanni nodded, 'Right, what's the plan? What do you want me to do with this pathetic guy?'

'Bring him back here pronto,' Declan commanded, adding. 'Unharmed, Giovanni.'

'You got it,' Giovanni said, pressing 'end' on his mobile phone before putting it back into his jacket pocket.

'Put him on the plane,' he said to his second in command who nodded. 'We're going home guys.'

An hour later, the man, fully restrained in chains and a mask to cover his mouth, was placed in a seat in front of Giovanni on the private plane that would take them all back to London.

Eyeing him with a sneer on his face, Giovanni coolly lit a cigarette and blew out a puff of smoke before opening his mouth to speak, 'So, you're the one responsible for my friend's death?'

The man winced slightly and tried to look away but his head was held forward, so that he was facing Giovanni.

'You work for Madge Sophokles. I presume you're like her go-to guy, right? She gets you to do her dirty work, like killing good people. Humans, Watchers, Guardians,' he thundered.

The man's fear-filled eyes skirted from Giovanni to the two empty seats beside him.

'You're gonna pay for what you've done. After the Watchers

have finished with you, they're gonna give you back to me,' Giovanni growled, allowing his eyes to glow a deep red.

The man swallowed loudly and a small bead of sweat slowly dripped off his forehead.

'Scared? You ought to be.'

The man made a sound through the mask.

Giovanni chuckled, 'He's scared, guys,' he said, momentarily looking away to laugh with his men.

When he looked back though, the whites of the man's eyes were completely black and before they had a chance to make a single move, what looked like a hole appeared right in front of them. Within seconds, the man was gone.

'Shit,' yelled Giovanni. 'A frickin' wormhole? You've got to be kidding me.'

He immediately got on the phone to tell Declan what had happened.

'... he could've gone anywhere. I don't understand either. I guess we should've covered his eyes. We never covered his eyes. Goddamnit,' Giovanni growled down the phone.

'We're on full alert in case he turns up here. Don't worry, we'll find him,' Declan reassured him, although his voice didn't sound quite so confident. 'Just get back here asap.'

$\maltese$ 25 $\maltese$

'We've got people out looking through all the tunnels beneath the city, but there's been no sign of her yet,' Declan said to Emma as they pored over a map of London.

'She's out there somewhere and that poor man is going to die if we don't reach her soon,' she said quietly.

'We need more information to speed this up,' he said. 'There's hundreds of miles worth of tunnels down there. We need something more to go on. I mean, the smell? It stinks everywhere down there.'

'Yeah I know,' Emma sighed. 'I wish I could give you more but the visions have stopped since I've been back. Any sightings of the other impostor?'

Declan screwed up his face and shook his head, trying hard not to yawn.

'You look exhausted, Declan. Maybe you should get some rest.'

His phone buzzed. Looking down, he smiled while reading a text.

'Saleena?' she asked.

Declan nodded.

'She, er, okay?'

'Fine, she's fine. She's a bit tired herself though. There's a lot going on at the moment and it's taking it's toll on all of us.'

'Look, why don't you go and spend a bit of time with her? We can cope here.'

But he shook his head. 'I'm no good to her like this, Emma. I can't rest until we've found Aria and John safe and sound. And then of course there's the escaped Skull as well as the other impostor in the infirmary down there,' he pointed downwards.

'Yeah I know.'

'And there's the funeral to organise too,' he said sadly.

'But we can't do that until we've sorted all this out. Most of the students don't even know the truth yet.'

Declan's eyes dropped towards the floor, 'I hate lying to them,' he muttered.

'I know, but it's for the best.'

'You know they're starting to ask questions. They want to see Eleanor.'

'Oh?' Emma said. 'Well, it's only natural, I suppose. She is,' she glanced up before continuing, '...was... a big part of their-our- lives. They're eager to see her again, make sure she's... okay,' Emma's voice broke.

'Hey, it's okay. Just remember what she said to you. She's happier now than ever.'

'Yeah, dead,' she sobbed.

'Don't cry, Emma. She asked us not to mourn her, remember? We are to remember all the good times we had with her.'

'Which is kind of difficult when there's someone down there that looks exactly like her...' Emma suddenly stopped.

'What's up?' asked Declan as Lana suddenly burst into the room.

'Hey guys, any news?' she asked, Barber walking in behind her.

Both Emma and Declan shook their heads without even looking at her.

'What are you thinking, Emma?' he asked again.

'That maybe it's time we brought her out of the infirmary. Surely we need her to think her plan has worked, right? We need to follow her every move, perhaps even bug her, you can read her mind, right? We can tell all the students in my class the truth and we can all do our thing to get to the bottom of this once and for all.'

'I'd thought about doing that before, but I'm having some difficulty with my mind reading abilities at the moment. I can't seem to read any minds since Canada, not really. It's like there's something preventing me, Emma. It's easier said than done,' Declan replied.

But Emma shook her head, 'If we work together, I think we can do it. We're pretty good actors when we put our minds to it, right? I'm sure it'll be okay without you reading everyone's mind,' she smiled for a second before adding, 'We can do this.'

'Emma's right, Declan. Don't you think it's time? That woman down there is going to be wondering why it's taking so long for her to be able to have her run of Praxos. Maybe it's time we gave it to her.'

'Perhaps you're right,' he said, sitting down at Eleanor's old desk.

'This still doesn't feel right,' he said, standing up again and sweeping his hand across the wood.

'That's because we haven't said a proper goodbye to Eleanor and the only way we can do that is by tricking that woman down there at her own plan,' Lana grinned.

Declan started to nod, a sly smile creeping across his lips.

'You know, girls. I think you're actually on to something. Gather the rest of the gang together. Bring them to...er...We need a good place to meet, somewhere well hidden.'

'How about somewhere that's hidden but isn't?' Emma suggested.

'Huh?' Lana said, squinting.

'The place where all of this began in the first place.'

'The Praxos pool?' Lana asked.

'No, I mean the place it ALL started for us. Our first introduction to Praxos.'

'Oh right, yes, what a great idea.'

Declan smiled while Barber crossed his arms and shrugged, wishing he could read minds.

❦ 26 ❦

'**W**elcome back, Eleanor!' everyone yelled as the impostor stepped into the great hall, finding hoards of students and teachers alike, all clapping, heralding the return of their dear Guardian.

She covered her eyes with her hands and cringed before attempting to smile at them all.

'Thank you,' she mouthed.

'Would you like to say anything to the students?' Declan smiled as he led her to the centre of the room where the famous Praxos statue stood. The impostor looked up at the huge angel holding a small child in her arms before noticing the plaque that read, Stamus Contra Malum.

Declan watched as the woman's expression turned, just briefly, to one of disgust. His fists clenched but he breathed deeply and smiled.

'No, I can't speak,' she whispered. 'Not well enough,' she said.

'Very well. I'll speak on your behalf,' he said, pushing her accidentally on purpose to one side.

'Hi folks. Thanks for coming out to welcome...' he stopped momentarily glancing towards Emma and her classmates before continuing, '...Eleanor... back to Praxos. Sadly, Eleanor's memory is still not complete so we must forgive her lack of knowledge about us all. However, physically, she is almost on form and hopefully soon will be back to her... former... self. So please give her some space to er, do her thing. She's still recovering. Welcome back... Eleanor,' he said the last word through gritted teeth, covering his mouth with his hands and forcing a cough while he stepped down.

The impostor stood, looking down at the expectant faces as they clapped and cheered, but she merely waved her hand very slightly and stepped down.

'Declan?' she asked as he went to walk away.

'Yes... Eleanor?'

'My memory,' she muttered. 'My office?'

'Of course, but wouldn't you rather get some rest?'

She shook her head, 'I presume there's a chair in my office?'

'Yes of course there is. Follow me,' Declan turned and headed off towards Eleanor's office.

Emma, Lana and the others from their class all smiled as she hobbled past.

'Witch,' muttered Lana under her breath after she'd disappeared into the room.

Declan returned to them and motioned for them to follow him. Walking down into the tunnel leading towards the lift they'd used when they'd first arrived at Praxos a few years before, Emma, Lana, Diarmuid, Ava and Moira all stepped into it while the others climbed the stairs beside it.

'Going up?' Lana joked as they stood, waiting for the lift to head upwards.

Stepping out, they all headed up towards the original living room where they'd first found out about Praxos. The living room was quite large with an inglenook fireplace and a number of sofas.

The students all made themselves comfortable as they watched the computer screen which had been positioned in the middle of the room. On it was a picture of Eleanor's office where the impostor sat at the desk.

'I hate this,' Lana murmured.

'Me too. It's so wrong,' said Diarmuid who was sitting with his hand on Emma's knee. 'I still can't believe she's really gone.'

'It only seems like yesterday that she was welcoming us all into Praxos,' sighed Elliott.

'She was a classy lady, Eleanor was,' Rupert smiled. 'Not like this filthy impostor here.'

'Do we know who it is yet?' asked Cassie who was sitting holding hands with Sammy.

Declan, who was standing with his arms crossed watching the screen intently, shook his head. 'But we reckon there's a good chance we're actually looking at Madge Sophokles.'

'No surprise there, really,' Penny sighed.

'When can we get the bitch?' Liam growled from the back of the room where he stood next to his girlfriend, Ava, who had her arm around his waist.

'All in good time, Liam,' Declan said. 'We need to lure her into a false sense of security first.'

'Do you think it's working?' asked Daisy who had just appeared with her father, Beau, in tow. 'Sorry we're a little late. Dad was just making sure all the bugs were in place.'

'Thanks Beau. How are you guys doing?'

'We're alright, I guess,' Beau replied, squeezing his daughter tight.

'Dad, I'm not a baby,' she smiled.

'Sorry sweetheart.'

'Has she done anything suspicious yet?' Daisy asked as she walked over to Sammy and Cassie and sat beside them on the sofa.

'Not yet,' Cassie sighed. 'She's just been sitting there rifling through all the desk drawers.

'Did you plant it, Declan?' Beau asked.

Declan grinned, 'Course.'

'What did you plant?' asked Emma.

'Just a few notes we wrote about Madge,' he smirked.

'Cool. I hope you were super nasty,' Lana said as they all turned their attention to the screen when they heard the woman grumbling under her breath.

'I guess she found them,' Beau said.

'And I guess this proves we are actually looking at Madge, then?' Emma asked.

'Guess so,' replied Declan. 'But let's not assume anything just yet.'

The impostor stood up and walked towards her office door.

Opening it slightly, she peered out, clearly making sure no-one was around. Content she was alone, she walked back to the desk and picked up the phone.

She looked at it for a second and then put it down.

'What's she doing?' asked Sammy. 'She doesn't know, does she?'

'Just give her time,' Declan reassured them.

Sure enough, the woman picked up the phone again and dialled.

'Are you getting that, Wilbur?' Declan asked.

One of the large closet doors opened, revealing Wilbur sitting at his own little desk, with headphones on. He gave a thumbs up sign.

Declan nodded.

'Hey. It's me,' the woman said.

Everyone in the room moved a little closer to the screen.

'I'm in,' she nodded. 'Of course not. They think I'm Eleanor. Really? You do realise I was a pretty good actress in my youth, you know,' she spat.

Emma clapped her hands and chuckled out loud.

'So busted,' she said. 'Madge said the exact same thing to me before. It's her, it's definitely Madge.'

'...you've what? Didn't she believe it was really her beloved? Are you totally useless? You can't even do one little thing I ask of you. All you had to do was to make them believe you were him. And now look, they're probably all wondering what happened to her. Oh Jesus, Stan...'

'Stan? It was Stan posing as John?' Lana breathed.

'And where is she now? You've what? Dumped her in the tunnel? And what about his body? The tunnel as well? Why would you do that? They're Watchers, Stanley Sophokles, they have special powers. What if they get out? Kill them? Of course you should kill them. We can't risk...'

Madge banged her hand on the desk, making the group jump.

'We're going to kill them all, Stan. Every last one of them. Why do you think I created this crazy plan in the first place? We were both supposed to get into Praxos posing as Eleanor and John and then we were going to kill them all. But if she figured out you weren't him, then...she didn't tell anyone did she? Of course it's a bloody good job you stopped her in time! Well, I shall just have to do this on my own. What about Valentine? Has he not checked in? And you can't reach him in Canada?'

Madge took a deep breath before continuing. 'Well yes, that is strange. He's usually very reliable, considering how desperate he is,' she tapped on the desk. 'Of course they haven't found him. Because if they'd found him, they'll have found her body, wouldn't they? My God, boy, you are damn stupid sometimes. I'm here aren't I? I've got the run of this place. You just do the one other job you were supposed to be doing and go and kill those two. I'll speak to you soon. I love you too, son,' Madge put the phone back on the desk and shook her head. 'Stupid boy,' she whispered.

'Yeah, totally stupid,' Liam said. 'He clearly takes after his mother.'

'Wilbur, do you have a location?'

Wilbur gave another thumb's up and took off his headphones.

'Looks like we're off, folks. You ready?' Declan asked.

Everyone jumped up and nodded.

'Let's do this. Beau, Sammy, Wilbur and Barber you guys stay here and guard this place. Make sure that Madge doesn't do a disappearing trick on us.'

Beau nodded, 'You can count on us, Dec. Good luck. Bring them home safe.'

'That's exactly what we're going to do,' he smiled, patting Beau on the back as he walked past.

Before they left, Wilbur gave Declan the last known whereabouts of Stan Sophokles.

'I'll keep you posted,' he said. 'Good luck.'

27

'I ...knew... you... could do it,' John croaked as Aria very carefully tried to lift her fiancé so that he could lean against the wall, and sit a little closer to the fire she'd managed to create.

'That better?' she asked as he nodded very slowly.

'I'm sorry,' he whispered.

'For what? For this? This isn't your fault, my darling.'

'You've...lost...years...'

'That's not important. The only thing that matters now is for us to get out of here and for you to get better. We've got our whole lives together now that I've found...'

Aria quickly realised they were no longer alone when the sound of footsteps began to get closer. Clapping echoed all around them.

'Why ain't that lovely. A reunion of the two lovebirds. Too bad it's not gonna last,' said the voice in the darkness. 'Quite romantic that your final moments will be together.'

'No,' whispered Aria. She touched John's hand to offer him some reassurance before she slowly stood up, the chains chafing against her wrists as she tried to pull herself away from the wall.

'You're not going to get away with this,' she said, coughing slightly.

'No? I think you're wrong there sweetheart. You're both gonna die and rot down here. No-one will ever find you. I'll make sure of that.'

But Aria laughed nervously. 'You must be more stupid than I thought.'

Detecting her nerves, Stan chuckled under his breath. 'How do you think you're going to survive, Aria? Your boyfriend is practically dead and you're chained to the pipes. I know you have no real Watcher powers otherwise you would have used them on me back at your place, instead of allowing yourself to be hit over the head with a frying pan.'

Aria rolled her eyes, he didn't even know the difference between a frying pan and saucepan. Not that it mattered now. Plus he hadn't even noticed she'd made a fire.

'Yes well, that was before,' she hissed.

'Before what?' he said, stepping a little closer so that the flames illuminated his face. He looked different from before. John's features were fading and it was becoming quite clear who this man was.

'Stan? I should have known it was you,' Aria said through gritted teeth.

'You mean you hadn't figured it out yet?' he burst out laughing. 'And I always thought you were quite bright. Shows how wrong I was.'

'You're quite often wrong about a lot of things,' she replied.

'Now, now sweetheart. You're not my stepmother anymore, you know.'

'I was never your stepmother, you vile creature.'

'Well, technically that's not true. You did marry my father.'

Aria breathed in deeply as she heard John gasp from beside her. 'You married...his father?'

'It's a long story, my love,' Aria whispered. 'I did it to find you. It was the only way I could find out the truth.'

'And you couldn't even do that, could you Aria?' Stan said as he lit a cigarette.

John coughed loudly beside her and she crept down, 'Forgive me, my love. It was all I could do. I will explain everything to you once we're out of this mess. I promise,' she whispered.

'Don't make promises you can't keep. You'll both be dead soon.'

'Like hell we will,' Aria shouted, clasping her hands together and doing all she could to muster more flames to throw at him.

But he was just about able to dodge them, disappearing out of sight.

'Oh, so you do have powers? After all this time, you managed to hide them well. I must say I'm impressed. Fire, huh? Shame you can't control it.'

'Yes I can,' she shouted again before she threw another couple of fireballs towards him.

Both he dodged easily, laughing as he hopped from one foot to the other like a professional boxer before he rushed forward towards her.

'Nice,' he said. 'But not nice enough.'

Before she knew what had happened, she felt a horrendous pain in her hand. Looking down, she realised she was bleeding. He'd sliced her with a knife.

'Aria?' croaked John from her side.

'I'm fine,' she answered, as she scoured around them, searching the semi-darkness for Madge's wretched son as he disappeared again.

'Where are you?' she screamed but he made no sound.

Then all of a sudden, she felt another blade slice into her arm.

'Aaarrgh.'

'Aria? No,' John cried.

'Don't worry. She'll be dead soon,' Stan whispered from further into the darkness. 'And then she'll be pain free,' he laughed before lunging forward again to cut her for the third time.

But this time she was ready. She pushed her hands forward, letting his blade hit the chains. He cursed loudly and she used that split second to throw another fire ball in his direction.

Watching, she grinned as it hit him in the lower leg, but he was back within seconds, his blade slicing and slicing through her skin.

She screamed, once, twice, as blood began to pour from her arms.

'Aria, no,' John sobbed from the floor. He tried to pick himself up, he needed to protect her, but his body wouldn't respond. He was far too weak. He could barely move. Sobbing, he tried to see what was happening, but his eyesight was so poor from years of being in captivity, in the darkness. 'Aria?' he whispered when it was silent for a moment.

Nobody said a word.

'Aria? Please... answer... me,' he croaked.

'No luck, mate?' Stan said from across the tunnel. 'I told you she'd be dead soon. Looks like she might already be gone. No-one can survive that kind of blood loss,' he laughed, wincing. His leg, severely burnt, was causing intense pain. Leaning against the wall, he took a deep breath, trying to control it. Listening as he did so, he grinned. He could hear nothing except for John's shallow breaths.

'Breathing a bit dodgy there, mate? Sounds like you've not got long either. Well, at least you'll be together forever. That is what you both wanted, right?' he laughed as he pushed himself up off the wall and turned to start limping away. 'Enjoy eternity down here.'

A few steps further and he took in a sudden breath of his own when a massive fireball hit him squarely in the back. Before he collapsed onto his knees, he just about managed to turn around.

'Eternity down here? I don't think so,' Aria yelled. 'Enjoy hell.'

She watched as the flames engulfed his body, his eyes bulging in terror and shock before his knees buckled and he collapsed fully onto the floor. The flames continued burning brightly, feeding off the body fat, sizzling quietly in the dark until eventually, they had nothing left to burn.

Aria, now collapsed into a heap next to John, watched every last second until her eyes could no longer remain open. Closing them, she let out a long deep, breath, 'John...'

28

'There!' screamed Emma. 'It's just down there, I recognise this.'

The others followed closely behind.

'Be careful,' Declan said, pulling her towards him. 'Let me go ahead. Stay behind me, you hear?'

Emma nodded and allowed him to get one step in front.

'That smell though. It's not the same smell,' she said. 'It smells like... burning.'

'Not just burning,' Lana whispered. 'That's burning flesh.'

'Shhhh,' Emma said. 'He could be here.'

'No,' Declan suddenly yelled, speeding up. 'He's not. He's gone.'

'What do you mean, Declan?' someone shouted from the back of the group. What do you mean, gone?' they asked as they ran down the long dark tunnel, using torches to light the way.

'He's dead, guys. We're safe. We just need to get there as quickly as possible,' he muttered.

'But how do you know, Declan?' someone asked.

'I can feel it. But I'm picking up on something else...something's wrong, they need help and they need it now.'

'Barber, get Emma down there fast.'

Before Emma could even register what was happening, Barber had lifted her into his arms and was running at almost the speed of light.

Emma squealed at the sight of the barely there fire and the two bodies beside it.

'Aria?' she yelled as Barber put her down. 'John?'

Neither responded.

'Barber, I need Diarmuid and I need him now. You need to go get him as fast as possible.'

Barber nodded and disappeared.

Emma concentrated on creating more light from within so she could get a good look at the two people.

Aria was covered in blood. Both were unconscious.

She placed one hand on each of them. Her fingers spread wide over their hearts, she focussed her entire being on healing them. But she needed Diarmuid to help. She couldn't save them both alone. Seconds later, she let out a deep breath as Barber appeared with her boyfriend on his back.

Diarmuid immediately let go and ran towards them.

'Emma?' he asked.

'They're both so close to dying, Diarmuid. I need to focus all my efforts on one at a time. Can you keep one alive so I can do this?'

Diarmuid nodded and placed both his hands on John's chest. Closing his eyes, he rocked very slowly back and forth until a bright golden aura encased them.

In the meantime, Emma did the same. Placing both her hands on Aria's body, she closed her eyes and breathed deeply. With one hand on her heart and the other on her forehead, Emma whispered quietly to herself until a bright golden aura covered them both.

From deep within the tunnel, the others began to emerge. They walked slowly towards the fire, watching as the miracle unfolded in front of them.

In front was Lana with her fingers in her mouth, holding her breath.

'Breathe Lana,' Declan whispered as he stepped beside her. 'We found them.'

Lana nodded as she turned to face him and smiled sadly. 'We did.'

'Let's hope they can save them,' Declan replied before returning his attention to the two healers.

'They can. I have every faith in them,' she whispered as she slowly walked forward until she stood next to Barber. He looked down, saw her shiver, and pulled her towards him.

She smiled and hooked her arms around him.

'They might not have made it in time if you hadn't been here, you know?'

Barber smiled. 'But I was here, and I'm not going anywhere.'

'I know,' Lana grinned. 'I have it on good authority that you're here to stay.'

Barber's eyebrows twitched and he shook his head in confusion, a slight chuckle escaping his lips.

'Thank you,' Lana whispered, holding him even tighter.

The two of them were joined by the rest of their classmates, who all just stood quietly watching the healers, praying that Aria and John would both survive. All in awe at witnessing this incredible duo in front of them. Diarmuid and Emma, the greatest healers Praxos had ever seen.

oOo

IT WAS ONLY AFTER ANOTHER HALF AN HOUR THAT DIARMUID finally released his hands from John's chest. the aura hovered around them both for a few seconds longer and then vanished into nothing.

DIARMUID BENT HIS HEAD TO LISTEN, SIGHING LOUDLY AT THE sound of a stronger heartbeat beneath his ears.

He sat back for a moment, breathing in and out through his mouth before he moved closer to Emma.

'Can I help?' he whispered.

She nodded and glanced towards Aria's arms, both full of slash marks from Stan's blade.

Diarmuid nodded and lifted one of her arms. Carefully placing his hand over the top of the cuts, he winced and turned back towards Emma.

'Poison?' he asked.

'A poisoned blade,' she replied.

The others listened and watched from where they sat on the floor, just a metre or so away from them.

'He sliced her with a poisoned knife?' Declan asked, as he paced back and forth.

Emma nodded, not taking her hands away from Aria's chest or head.

'It's pretty bad,' she sighed. 'Her heartbeat is getting a little stronger, though' she tried to smile. 'But I think we're going to need the antidote for her to make a full recovery.'

Declan nodded and searched the ground for the blade.

'What happened to the knife he used?' he asked.

'The ashes,' Lana whispered. 'It's in the ashes.'

'What ashes? asked a few of the voices.

Lana released her grip on Barber and stepped further away from them, moving as if in a trance.

'Lana?' asked Declan. 'You alright mate?'

But she said nothing, she just continued to walk further away until she stopped in front of something on the ground.

'Here,' she pointed, looking down. 'The blade.'

Declan rushed to her side and bent down. His fingers touched the ashes containing the ancient looking dagger.

'It's him,' Declan said, standing up with the knife in his hands.

'Who?' asked Barber.

'Stan.'

'What do you think happened to him? Barber asked.

Lana bent down and gingerly allowed her fingers to make contact with his remains. She cringed, closing her eyes for a moment before she slowly returned to her feet. Smiling, she turned towards the others and did a fist-pump.

'Aria, you're amazing,' she smiled before explaining what had happened between Stan and Aria.

'How do you know? Did you have a vision just now?' asked one of her classmates.

'Yeah,' she smiled. 'I saw everything.'

'I don't suppose he said anything about Madge or that Valentine guy?'

She shook her head, 'Sorry, no.'

Declan nodded. Well, at least we've annihilated one of them.'

$\text{❧}\quad 29\quad\text{❧}$

Later that evening, Sammy walked into the room containing the two patients and asked, 'How are they doing?'.

'John is recovering well, but it's going to take quite a while for him to regain his strength. He's also going to need some counselling, I think,' Emma replied as they walked over to the bed and pulled a thicker blanket over him.

'Has he regained consciousness yet?'

'Briefly.'

'Did he say anything?' asked Sammy.

'He just wanted to know if Aria was going to live. When I told him the truth,' he thanked me and went straight back out.'

'You told him the truth?'

Emma nodded, 'Sammy, he has a right to know that she might not make it.'

'Yeah, I guess. Any news on the antidote?'

Emma slowly shook her head, 'But we've got our best people on it.'

'And how is she doing?' Sammy walked over towards Aria and looked down at her bandaged arms.

'She's strong, I'll give her that, but this poison is something else. If it's in her bloodstream for much longer, I'm afraid she won't be able to survive it'.

'And we have no idea where the poison came from?'

Emma shook her head as she adjusted the IV drip.

Sammy looked on in amazement, 'How do you know all this stuff? It's like you're a fully qualified nurse or something.'

'I just do,' she shrugged. 'But I will be going to medical school as well.'

'You will?' Sammy asked as they walked out of the room and closed the door behind them. This led them directly into the living room which had been set up to spy on Madge.

'It was such a good idea to create a makeshift infirmary here,' Sammy smiled.

'Well, we couldn't have them anywhere Madge would find them. Plus, we had to keep them away from all the other students. Although I still feel awful lying to everyone about all this.'

'Yes but we must continue this charade until we've found Valentine,' Declan interrupted.

He was sitting eating a sandwich watching Madge on the screen. 'Until we find him, we have to continue pretending.'

'Yeah but we've got John and Aria back now. Surely we can just lock her up and throw away the key?' Sammy asked, moving to sit beside him.

But Declan shook his head, dropping a little bit of banana on his shirt.

'Is that a banana sandwich?' Sammy grinned.

'My favourite,' he smiled, offering her a bite.

She shook her head, 'I used to eat those when I was a little kid.'

He chuckled and continued, 'As long as Valentine is out there, we can't risk it. He could use his wormhole to rescue her. We've got to nail him before we do anything. Only when we have him, can we finally move on.'

'It kinda sucks,' Sammy sighed, leaning back in the chair.

'I agree, but some things in life do suck. And we just have to go with it for a while.'

Sammy nodded, watching Emma as she sat on the sofa with a cup of tea in her hands.

'You okay, Emma?'

With her eyes closed, she sighed and nodded. 'Just a bit tired.'

One of the doors suddenly burst open and Lana appeared, breathless.

'I just got word from one of the witches, the poison, it's tree-based.'

'Tree-based? What does that even mean?' asked Daisy, who had been sitting on the floor reading a book about ghosts.

Sammy's ears pricked.

'It means that Sammy might be the key to this,' Lana answered. 'Ready to go talk to some trees, Sam?' she grinned.

'Sure,' she said, jumping up off the chair and following Lana out of the room.

'Which trees?'

'That's the problem. We're not sure.'

Sammy nodded, 'Er... okay. I'll do everything I can. Lead the way.'

$$\text{❧} \quad 3 \, 0 \quad \text{❧}$$

Standing at the foot of an ancient tree with huge branches
jutting out from it's twisted trunk, Sammy smiled. It was
one of her most favourite trees that she'd discovered since
moving to London over a year ago. Located in the middle of
Epping Forest, it was easy enough to get to from the centre of the
city; especially when you had all of Praxos' transportation at hand.

Lana stood by her side, quietly doing nothing but watching on
as Sammy prepared to communicate with the great example of
such an old species of plant-life. With her arms outstretched,
Sammy leaned in, allowing herself to fully embrace the gnawed
trunk. Smiling, she sighed.

As always, the tree was overjoyed to have a human to communicate with and Sammy could almost feel it return her embrace.

Closing her eyes, she began to hum for a moment. Lana, feeling
a little silly just standing in the middle of the forest clearing,
searched for and found a low tree stump to sit on. Perching on it,
she closed her eyes and sighed, enjoying the gentle reverberations
of Sammy's voice. Suddenly, she felt herself fall and so quickly
opened her eyes with her arms outstretched, worried she would
hurt herself. But it was clear she was no longer sitting in the forest
clearing. In fact, she had no idea where she was at all.

Trapped within a circular, perpendicular tunnel, she could just
about feel the walls all around her.

It was rough, damp and smelt exactly like the place she'd just been standing. Listening, the sound of Sammy's humming had grown louder. It was dark but when she looked upwards, she noticed little patches of light twinkling through a few holes above her.

Again, the humming grew louder and louder until Lana was able to make out words responding to her. She was in the tree!

'Sammy? Sammy, can you hear me?' she breathed.

But Sammy said nothing, she just continued humming.

'It's just a vision, nothing more,' Lana whispered to herself, realising she should just go with the flow and listen.

As she calmed down and stood, she let her hands stroke the inside of the trunk while listening intently to the words of the tree.

'Welcome back, my friend. It is always such a pleasure to have you here on the forest floor with us. I understand you require our assistance? Oh no, that's terrible, my friend. Poisoned, you say? Why ever would anyone wish to do such a thing? Evil? Yes, that's true. They must be evil. Of course. How can we assist you, my friend? Poison from a fellow tree? Oh dear. Why yes, but not from around these parts. You would need to travel far and wide, across the vast blanket of water, to obtain what you require to save her. You say you were in a country far from here? Yes I believe what you require can only be found there, my dear. You must obtain the sap from the place it was taken and mix it with a number of ingredients to save her life. The ingredients? Why yes of course. The sap is the crucial element, then you must add a dash of Ricinus Communis, a hint of Foxglove Digitalis, a most minute amount of Atropa Belladonna and several pinches of maple syrup for good measure. Your patient must ingest this soon, my dear, for she will not survive much longer with the poison in her bloodstream. Good luck, my friend. Be well. Return when you can...'

The words returned to simple humming and when Lana opened her eyes, she was sitting on the tree trunk watching Sammy remove her hands from the beautiful tree that had been so eager to help.

'I know what we need,' Sammy said. 'But we're going to need some help from our people in Nova Scotia.'

Lana nodded, 'I know.'

Sammy looked up at her and screwed her eyebrows together. 'You do?'

'I had a vision and I heard him talking to you.'

'Cool,' Sammy replied, 'But you mean her, not him,' she giggled as the two walked quickly back to the car where the driver was waiting patiently for them.

'Ring Declan,' Lana instructed. 'He'll know who to call.'

Sammy got straight on to the phone to tell Declan everything about what the tree had suggested before she turned her attention back to Lana.

The car came to a temporary standstill in traffic when Sammy asked, 'What happened in your vision then, Lana?'

Smiling, she turned to Sammy and explained everything she'd seen and heard.

'You were actually inside the tree?'

Lana nodded, 'It was really weird, but yes. I know the tree wasn't physically talking to you but I could understand the words and your humming too. It was really, erm, special.'

Sammy grinned, 'It is special. I'm lucky I have this talent.'

'And to be able to talk to animals too, that's insanely cool. I'm officially jealous.'

'Well, I wish I could do what you and Emma do.'

'Your power is just as cool, if not cooler,' Lana reassured her but Sammy shook her head.

'I'd be useless in a fight though. You and Emma are really good at kicking butt, as well as being able to jump from huge heights or swim underwater for ages.'

'Well, I can't swim underwater for long periods of time.'

'But Emma can breathe for you as well though, can't she?'

Lana nodded, 'she has done that before when we've done our underwater vision thing.'

'How?' Sammy asked.

'She creates a sort of oxygen bubble that envelopes us, not that she needs it. She can breathe in the water. But she makes a bubble for anyone that can't.'

'See? Totally cool.'

'She is pretty cool, my sister,' Lana sighed, sitting back. 'She's an incredible healer too. That's what she's going to do with her life, you know?'

Sammy nodded, 'Yeah, it's clear to see that. But what about you? Have you decided what you're going to do when we finish our studies?'

Lana shrugged, 'I've been told I'll do a lot of travelling and continue working for Praxos.'

'Well, we'll all continue working for Praxos, won't we?' Sammy suddenly asked, unsure.

'I guess so. I never really thought about it before. Don't you have any idea what you want to do, Sammy?'

'I thought about becoming a veterinarian? Would Praxos ever need a vet though? I'm not sure,' she shrugged.

'Yes of course. I mean what if something were to happen to Giovanni or any of the other werewolves, for example, while they were in wolf form? They'd need a vet to help them, right?'

'Oh yeah,' Sammy smiled. 'Sounds a bit scary though.'

Lana laughed, 'Maybe, but you could handle it, Sammy. I think it's a great idea. You should talk to Eleanor about it,' she said, glancing out of the window.

'Don't you mean Declan, Lana?' Sammy said sadly.

'Yeah, isn't that what I said?'

Sammy shook her head, 'You said Eleanor.'

Both girls looked down for a second.

'I guess it still hasn't sunk in,' Lana muttered.

'It'll take time for all of us,' Sammy whispered.

‎❧ 31 ❧

'We've got eyes on the house in Nova Scotia, but as yet have detected no movement there at all,' Giovanni said over the phone to Declan. 'Anything your end?'

Looking out across the Thames from his houseboat, Declan shook his head.

'Nothing, nada, zip. We're beginning to think he's just done a runner.'

'I doubt that. Madge will have him holed up somewhere preparing for some big hit. What's our next move?' he asked, taking a packet of cigarettes out of his jacket pocket while holding the phone precariously between his head and shoulder.

'Well, we're still keeping a close eye on Madge, but she's not given anything else away. She has tried calling Stan a couple of times and is getting increasingly angry at his lack of response though. She might do something stupid as a result,' he stated.

'Yeah, and if she does, we'll be ready. How's Aria doing?'

'Not too good, I'm afraid. But we might be onto something with the antidote though. We've got a couple of our witches brewing something up. We just need one special ingredient from Nova Scotia, sap from a tree. We reckon it must be from one of the trees where the bodies were found. We could do with the wormhole to get it here faster,' Declan sighed.

'Would be handy, wouldn't it? But yeah, I heard that some of our guys were in the woods collecting something this morning. They should be with you soon. Well, let me know if there's anything I can do to help.'

'Will do, Giovanni,' Declan sighed. 'And...'

'Yeah?'

'Thanks mate.'

'No problem. I'd do anything for you guys.'

Declan smiled as he put the phone down and glanced across at the London Eye, watching it slowly rotate in the distance.

'Dec, babe?' said a voice from below deck.

'Right here, Sal. What's up?'

'I'm going to sleep for a little while, please lock up when you go out.'

'Sleeping again? You still tired, love?' he asked as he hopped down the steps and followed her into the bedroom.

His beautiful Indian girlfriend just smiled as she laid down on the bed.

'Are you sure you're alright?' he asked, putting his hand to her forehead.

'I'm fine. You just go and finish this so we can get back to normal,' she told him.

'I don't think it's ever going to be back to normal but...'

'You know what I mean,' she smiled, stroking his cheek softly.

'Just put an end to this horrible episode so life can go on the way it should. Poor Eleanor needs to be laid to rest. It's time, Declan.'

'I know, love. It is time. We're doing everything we can to sort this out. Look, you sure you're okay? I can stay if you like?'

'Baby, you can't stay and I'm fine anyway. Just finish this once and for all and then come back to me and we can live our lives, okay? Promise me?'

Declan smiled, leaning over her. He nodded and kissed her on the lips.

'I promise, Sal. This will all be over soon. Get some shut eye, then. I'll lock up. Love you, babe.'

Saleena smiled and closed her eyes.

'I love you too, Declan. Now go and get those bad guys. And be careful.'

Declan stood over her for a few minutes, just until her breathing slowed and he could see she was gently sleeping. With his brow furrowed, he sighed, wondering what it was she was blocking from him. Lately, he felt like everyone was blocking something from him. He was unable to fully read what some of the others were thinking and it was worrying him. Was it something Madge had done to him in Canada?

Shaking it off, he turned away and climbed out of the boat, locking up behind him, just as he'd promised before he headed back to Praxos.

Walking through the streets of London, he started to get a funny feeling someone was watching him. He stopped for a moment, pretending to do up his shoelace, instead focussing on all the people within close proximity. Regular people were milling around, tending to their daily business. One man though, seemed different to everyone else. Declan couldn't see him, but he could sense him. His thoughts, however, were blocked off.

Standing up and straightening his jacket, he turned left at the lights, continuing on until he reached the corner of Bloomsbury Square where he took a seat in one of the benches. Leaning back, he crossed one ankle over his knee and looked around. He took his phone out of his pocket and began pretending he was texting. Instead though, he turned the camera back on himself so he could see behind him. There was nobody there. So he turned off the camera and made a phone call.

Five minutes later, he received a text.

'We're here.'

Declan replied immediately, 'Anything?'

'Give us a minute.'

Two minutes passed and another text arrived.

'Young male. 25ish. Odd-looking.'

Declan read it and replied, 'Odd-looking how?'

'Like he's from another era.'

'Must be him. Keep on his tail,' Declan pressed send and stood up, rubbing his hands together for a moment to warm them up. He turned and surreptitiously had a good look around, spotting Barber and Lana acting like a young couple in love, sneakily keeping an eye on a man who was clearly pretending to read a newspaper.

Not wanting to alert suspicion, Declan winked at Lana when he was out of sight and continued walking towards Praxos.

Lana and Barber watched as the man stood up from the wall he'd been leaning against and continued walking. They discreetly followed behind. When Declan arrived at the main Praxos entrance, they watched as the man stopped for a moment before he carried on walking straight past. They followed him, but once he turned the corner, he vanished.

'The wormhole,' Lana breathed.

32

'So you think he followed you to find out where Praxos is?' asked Emma.

Declan nodded.

'But he must know where it is. He was here before, right? When Madge got inside when she first took Eleanor?'

'Yes but maybe he doesn't realise it's the same place? Maybe he's as dumb as Stan and Madge put together?'

'Well that wouldn't surprise me. But what do you think he's doing? Why is he trying to get in?'

'Because he needs to tell Madge that we know the truth. She can't reach him, can she?'

'Oh yeah, I suppose not. So what are we going to do?'

'Well, we need to catch him before he can create another wormhole. Once we've got him, then we can finally put Madge where she belongs. But we can't risk doing that until we've actually got him. It would be hell if he escaped again with her.'

'What's the plan?' she asked, as she began to help the other nurses administer the antidote to Aria.

'How do we stop him from making another wormhole when we catch him?'

'That's the all important question,' he replied. 'How's she doing?'

'Honestly? I really don't know. We're totally relying on this stuff to get her through this. If this doesn't work, then it's unlikely she'll... make it,' she whispered, glancing over at John's bed as he slept fitfully.

Declan nodded. 'It'll work, Emma. It'll work. It's got to.'

'I hope you're right.'

'How's John doing?'

'He's been awake a few times but we've been giving him stuff to help him sleep. He'll heal quicker in his sleep,' she said as they walked over to his bed. 'But he's clearly recalling much of what's happened while he's dreaming,' she sighed, leaning over to adjust the blanket.

'Well, that's only natural. He was kidnapped ten years ago. It's going to take its toll. Poor bloke.'

'I've spoken to a few of our counsellors and they're confident Praxos will help him heal quicker than, well, regular folk.'

'You sound like you've been doing this job for years, Emma. I'm proud of you.'

'Thanks Declan,' she said, turning to leave the makeshift infir-mary with Declan by her side.

'I spoke to Patrick this morning,' Declan said, opening the door for her.

'How is Dad?' she asked, walking into the other room containing all the students who knew the truth.

'He's been worrying about you and Lana but, don't worry, I reassured him that you're both fine. Just super busy.'

Emma smiled, 'Thanks. And Mum, the kids?'

'All good, nothing to worry about. They all sent their love.'

Emma walked over to one of the side tables where tea, coffee and biscuits had recently been placed.

'I'm dying for a cup of tea. Can I pour a cup for anyone else,' she asked, turning to hand one of the mugs to Declan as she poured coffee into it while he stood waiting.

'Thanks, mate,' he sighed, taking a long sip and returning his attention to the computer screen.

'Where's Madge?' he asked when he noticed she wasn't in Eleanor's office.

'She just left,' Wilbur answered, turning to face another of the screen's in his little cubby hole office. 'And she's headed to the white room.'

'Keep watching,' Declan instructed.

'She's got a phone in her hand,' Wilbur added. 'Presumably she's going to try and make another call. Don't worry, I'm way ahead of you, Declan.'

Wilbur increased the volume on one of the screens as they all stopped what they were doing and leaned in to watch as Madge dialled a number.

'It's the same number again,' Wilbur said.

'Stan's probably.'

They watched as Madge began pacing back and forth in the white room. Suddenly, she picked up a water bottle and threw it across the room. The glass shattered on impact with the wall.

'Oh dear, looks like the pressure's getting to her,' Liam sniggered. 'When are we going to take this bitch down?'

'All in good time, Liam. All in good time.'

'Not soon enough,' Liam replied, clenching his fists.

'You're so ready for a fight, aren't you,' Lana said to her former boyfriend.

'Aren't you?' he questioned.

'Well yeah I guess so. But Declan's right. We must get the timing right.'

'I know,' Liam muttered under his breath.

'We'll get her, babe,' said Ava, putting her arm over his shoulder as he sat back down in the chair.

All continued watching as two of the younger students rushed into the white room.

'Eleanor, erm, miss Hayden-Jones? Are you alright?' asked one of them, walking to her side, while the other went over to the smashed glass on the floor.

'Don't worry, Miss. I'll clean this up. Can I get you another bottle of water?'

Eleanor growled loudly.

The young student next to her took two tentative steps away.

'Oh dear, looks like she's going to lose it,' Liam smiled, leaning forward to watch the screen.

But before she did anything more, Eleanor shook her head and stepped backwards.

'No, I'm...I'm... fine. Just... just... clean it up...' she grumbled and quickly exited the room and rushed back to the office.

'Bloody hell, what's up with Eleanor?' asked the young student near the door.

'Dunno, but I've never seen her like that before. I guess her kidnapping has left a black mark on her soul,' said the other as he bent down and started picking up the broken glass.

'Left a black mark on her? We need to put an end to this soon,' Emma sighed. 'It's awful that we're allowing Madge free rein throughout Praxos. Those poor students think that it's really Eleanor. We can't allow this to go on, Declan. We can't let Eleanor's legacy be tainted like this.'

'Once we've cracked this, Emma. The students will know the whole truth. Nobody will remember Eleanor any other way than the way she should be remembered. But we have to do this right. We have to take her and this Valentine fella down properly. For once and for all. We can't give them any chance of escape. It's coming, though. Don't worry about that. They're going down.'

❧ 33 ☙

Once Valentine had realised that Madge's plan had been thwarted, he decided to work out a new one. One that Madge would approve of. One that would finally give him what he wanted. To return home. Home to the 17th Century.

Madge was the only person who could help him, she'd been the one to pull him from his life in the first place. He'd always known he was capable of hopping from one place to another using his wormhole skill but never had he hopped through time. Until that fateful Sunday when Madge had summoned him. Not knowing what or who was calling him from yonder, he'd created his usual wormhole, thinking he would simply travel to another part of the west country county where he lived but, no, he'd travelled across hundreds of years to land in this blessed place where the world had changed beyond recognition. He hated it, every part of it and he wanted to go back. Madge was his only hope.

And so he would do everything possible to get her out of Praxos, to free her, and him at the same time. He'd already carried out one brief recce of the academy and was preparing to do a second when he saw the man who had caught him in Nova Scotia. Giovanni was his name.

Watching from the distance, he saw him confidently cross the road and down the steps into the Praxos Academy. The man frightened him a little, but although Giovanni might have come across all macho and violent, he had been easy to escape from.

Valentine shook his head as he scoured the area behind him. Giovanni had entered the place alone.

Walking across the road, he put up the hood on his jumper, the ridiculous item of clothing he'd been forced to wear to blend in with the rest of the crowd, and looked down the steps.

He knew there were several entrances to Praxos, but this was the one open to the public. He'd learnt that it was a faux entrance, posing as an alternative entrance to the university building next door. Unfortunately, using the wormhole was no longer a possibility within Praxos. When it had been used the first time round, Madge had made sure their guards had been down. Now though, it was practically impossible to enter this way. He had no choice but to enter the old fashioned way. He had to just walk in, find Madge and walk out. Not an easy feat but one he was confident he could carry out. It was, after all, his only way of returning home.

34

The first blast sounded like thunder. Moments later, the second sounded exactly like what it was, an explosion.

The second it became clear what was happening, Declan immediately set about locating Madge.

'What's happening,' yelled Emma from the adjoining makeshift infirmary, as she ran into the room.

'An explosion,' Declan said, 'You stay here with Aria and John. I'll leave Wilbur with you. The others are coming down with me.'

Emma nodded, 'Be careful,' she rushed back, locking the door behind her and making sure the patients and the other nurses stayed safe.

'Do you reckon it's Valentine?' asked Lana as the group ran down the stairs, avoiding using the elevator in case the power went down.

'It must be,' Declan turned to look at her. 'He's trying to get in or he's trying to get her out. Our number one priority right now is locating Madge and stopping him from taking her. If you find him, you must cover his eyes. It's his eyes that work the wormhole. Got me?' he asked, as he turned to run towards Eleanor's office.

Lana nodded, pulling Barber, Diarmuid, Liam and Rupert with her.

'Boys, we've got to find Valentine.'

'It's about time,' growled Liam eagerly.

As they arrived at the main Praxos hall, Lana looked around amidst the chaos of students rushing around everywhere. Glancing at the Praxos statue, she breathed a slight sigh of relief that it was still in one piece. It would break her heart to find it destroyed. Looking down one of the tunnels, she finally spotted what she was looking for. Valentine had used some kind of explosion to gain entry via the tunnels. Shaking her head, she pointed to the boys behind her.

'He's got to be here somewhere,' she shouted. 'Find him. Cover his eyes, boys.'

The others rushed around her, each one taking a different route to try and locate the man who had caused this commotion.

'Just one man did this?' asked Sammy, who had followed them down the stairs. 'There must be more than one, Lana. There must be.'

Lana listened while she scoured the area.

'Get to your dorm rooms,' she shouted to the younger students who were gathering in the hall. 'It's not safe here. Get to your dorm rooms now,' she yelled. 'Take your fellow students with you and stay there until we come and get you, okay?' she asked.

Some of the students began to nod, older ones getting the attention of the young students and ushering them away from the chaos.

Soon, the crowds began to disperse and it was easier to see the scale of destruction. Two of the tunnels had been partially obliterated, leaving falling pieces of concrete hanging precariously from above. Dust filled the great room. Lana coughed as she walked through, careful not to stumble on the debris.

As she approached Eleanor's office, she found Declan lying on the floor, a large sword stuck right through the centre of his chest.

She gagged and rushed to his side, 'Declan!' she screamed. 'No, no, no, no,' she murmured. 'How could you let this happen?'

Turning she found Madge sitting at Eleanor's desk with a smile on her face.

'You,' Lana breathed, slowly standing up to face her. 'You are responsible for this,' she pointed.

'Why yes, I suppose I am,' Madge replied, joy visible across her features.

'He was starting to get on my nerves, always getting in my business.'

'You've killed him,' Lana muttered, knowing full well Declan was only temporarily dead. His Praxos tattoo, Resurgam, meant 'I shall rise again', but Madge didn't know the truth so Lana went along with it.

'Eleanor, how could you? He was one of your closest friends? What happened to you?'

'I...I...well I... oh heck I've had enough of this. Stop calling me Eleanor. It's driving me mad. I hate that woman's name. You can call me...'

'Madge?' Lana said, bringing herself up to full height.

'You know?'

'You're not a very good actress.'

Madge's top lip lifted. 'I happen to be an amazing actress, you disgusting little wench.'

Lana raised her brow and turned quickly back to Declan.

'Sorry,' she whispered to him as she deftly pulled the sword from his body and returned her attention to Madge.

'We've known the truth for some time actually,' she smiled. 'We've watched everything you've done while you've been here. Having trouble reaching your son, have you? That's because he's dead. We killed him.'

'B...b...but he's my son. He can't be dead. You're bluffing.'

Lana smiled, gingerly taking a couple of steps closer to Madge, the sword carefully hovering between them both.

'Nope, he's going to burn in hell for eternity.'

'I don't believe you,' Madge said as she picked up a dagger from the desk, slowly stood up and moved towards the door.

'Oh no you don't,' Lana said, pointing the sword at her. 'Stay where you are, you evil cow. Valentine isn't getting anywhere near you.'

Madge's eyes opened wide, 'Valentine? This is the work of Valentine?'

Lana kicked herself for telling her too much information.

'Why, I never gave him enough credit. Valentine. Smarter than I realised.'

'Actually, he's not smart enough, breaking into Praxos? Stupid thing to do really,' Lana answered, brandishing the weapon in between them.

'We did it once before. Actually, technically you could say I did it twice, wouldn't you?'

Lana snarled, 'I've just about had enough of you.'

'Had enough have you?'

Madge suddenly dodged Lana's sword before stumbling over Declan's body on the ground. She fell to her knees.

Lana smiled and took the moment to lift the sword high, very tempted to swing it across the woman's neck when the door flew open.

'Lana!' shrieked one of the younger students. 'What are you doing to Eleanor?'

Taken by surprise, Lana temporarily let her guard down and Madge made her move, hopping up and out of the door, grabbing the youngster as she went.

Lana cursed under her breath and stood, watching as Madge held the dagger to her victim's neck.

'Eleanor?' the girl whispered before she looked across at Lana.

'Lana?' she squealed.

'Don't worry, you're going to be fine,' she reassured. 'Let her go, Madge.'

'Madge?' the girl whispered before she began to cry.

'Stop crying you stupid child,' Madge snarled as the girl shuddered beneath her fingers. 'Just shut up or I'll hurt you, badly. Actually, no. I'll probably kill you.'

The girl stopped shuddering, and looked up at Lana, the tears falling down her cheeks silently.

'Help me,' she pleaded silently.

❧ 35 ❧

Whilst Lana was busy trying to figure out the best way to save the young Watcher, the others were on the hunt for Valentine, who, as yet had evaded capture. In fact, he hadn't even been spotted.

'Anything?' asked Barber to Diarmuid as they almost collided with each other down one of the other tunnels.

Diarmuid shook his head, 'No sign. You?'

Barber gritted his teeth, 'Where the hell is he?'

'Maybe he keeps using the wormhole to get away?' Diarmuid suggested while Liam and Ava appeared behind them.

'We can't find him anywhere, we've looked high and low,' Ava breathed as the rest of her classmates rushed around the corner, slowing when they saw the group gathering together.

'Declan's dead,' she added. 'For now, anyway and...' she stopped for a moment to listen carefully before continuing, 'Madge is holding someone hostage. Lana is trying to release her.'

Liam stood beside her, clenching and unclenching his fists. 'Can you hear anything else?' he asked.

'Nothing of any substance,' she replied. 'Sorry guys, I just can't hear Valentine at the moment. I wish my power was stronger,' she sighed.

'Hey, don't beat yourself up, you're doing a good job,' said Rupert. 'I've been looking through all the walls in here and I can't see him either. He must be using the wormhole as a means of trav-elling around the place.'

'Let's concentrate on helping Lana. He'll show himself soon enough and we'll be ready,' Liam said. The others followed behind him, quietly approaching the main hall where Madge stood with a dagger to the throat of a young Watcher. Lana was facing the two of them, her face like thunder. When she spotted the others behind, she nodded discreetly.

'Hey,' shouted Liam to the older woman.

Madge turned, her eyes locking with his.

'Why don't you let her go. You know there's no way out of this?' Rupert called to her.

Madge stepped backwards slightly, pulling the girl closer to herself.

'I don't think so, I'm going to be out of here in no time.'

'Really?' asked Liam. 'You really think we're just going to let you walk out of here?' he laughed. 'You're even more stupid than we thought.'

Her eyes like slits, she let out a slight growl, gripping the dagger tighter.

The girl yelped as the blade made contact with the skin, causing a little blood to drip down her throat.

'Hey, no need to do anything rash,' Lana said, holding her hands up before putting the sword down on the floor. 'Just let her go.'

Madge chuckled, stepping back further. 'Come on Valentine, where are you?' she yelled, holding the blade firmly to the girl's throat.

The gang of Watchers immediately tensed, looking around to see if they could spot the elusive Skull, ready to stop him from taking her.

'Right here, Ma'am,' said a voice in the darkness.

Immediately Liam ran to where the sound had come from.

'I'll get him,' he growled under his breath. Catching sight of him, he smirked, ready to knock him out.

But seconds before Liam reached him, the man was gone.

'Shit,' Liam muttered. 'He's gone again,' he yelled from the darkness.

'No, I'm right here,' Valentine said from another corner of the room.

Barber immediately rushed to the darkness, but again, he was eluded by the young man.

'And here,' he yelled. 'Nope, I'm here. 'And here...and here... over here...this way...you'll never catch me. Just give me the woman and let us go. That's all I ask.

'Valentine, stop playing around and get me out of here,' Madge shrieked after about five minutes of the Watchers playing, and losing this game of catch.

But Valentine didn't re-appear.

'Valentine?' she asked. 'I said come and get me.'

But when he didn't answer, she grew impatient and stamped her feet.

Needing a moment to catch his breath, Valentine stood leaning back against the wall inside Eleanor's office. With his hands on his knees, he took a few deep breaths, ready to go back, ready to take what he needed to get home. She was his ticket. His only ticket.

Taking one last deep breath, he prepared to slip into the wormhole that would take him to her side. He needed a little more energy to carry more than one person so he took his time, letting the breath slip quietly from his lips. Just as he opened the wormhole to step through, he felt a deep thud, followed by an intense pain in his back. He fell into the hole with Declan falling close behind him.

A split second later, he appeared beside Madge, her face finally beginning to change.

'About bleeding time,' she snapped at him. 'Let's get out of...' but before she could finish the sentence, Declan appeared out of nowhere and, in what seemed like slow motion, gave Valentine a punch to the face. He fell to the ground like a rag doll.

Lana took immediate advantage and pounced on Madge, wrestling her against the Praxos statue as Declan stumbled backwards, his hands holding on to his chest, where he'd been sliced through with a sword earlier.

The young Watcher was desperately trying to get out of harm's way, watching as Declan fell to the ground, still too weak to continue the fight.

Liam and Ava immediately rushed to her side, pulling her out of the way, before the others swooped down on Valentine, covering his head with a black cover and carrying him away from Madge and Lana.

But unbeknown to the group, Madge did actually have her own Skull power. She was a pretty nifty fighter. Throwing punches left, right and centre, Lana was having to dodge the woman's attack, throwing her own punches whenever she had the chance.

Madge kicked out at her, catching Lana unawares. She fell backwards, stumbling onto the ground behind her. As she quickly stood up and regained her footing, Madge put her hands on her hips for a second, jubilantly enjoying her attack. Lana took the moment to fully bound towards the woman, leaving her no time to escape. Lana's head made full contact with Madge's stomach. The Skull was thrown backwards. Bashing her head into the Praxos statue, she fell with her head facing upwards.

The statue wobbled slightly and Madge, with her eyes wide open with terror, watched as the marble child fell from her mother's arms straight onto her head.

Lana lunged forward, catching the smaller statue as it bounced into her arms.

Silence filled the great room for just a moment and then, cheers raged, echoing around the whole of Praxos as hidden students and teachers began to appear from the darkness, rejoicing their victory.

❦ 36 ❦

The man sat in the corner of his cell, quivering beneath his mask.

'He's not so smug now is he?' asked Lana the following day.

Declan, who had fully recovered from his death, smiled. 'Nope, he isn't. But there's something weird about this guy. I can't quite put my finger on it.'

'Won't he speak?' asked Emma, who had entered the prison room with her sister just moments earlier.

Shaking his head, Declan crossed his arms. 'Not to me, not to Wilbur or Barber or any of the other teachers.'

'Can't you read his mind?' Lana queried.

'Sadly no,' he said, shaking his head. 'I haven't been able to really get into anyone's mind since the events in Nova Scotia, remember?.'

Both Lana and Emma gasped, 'What, still nothing? I thought it would have worn off by now,' Lana replied.

'You don't think it's permanent, do you?' asked Emma, clearly concerned.

'It's been a while since we were there and little has changed, mate. So yeah, I do.'

'Oh Declan, I'm so sorry,' she said.

'I'm not,' Lana smirked, joking. 'It wasn't nice having someone else in your head.'

Declan gently punched her on the shoulder.

'Hey,' she chuckled. 'What do we do now?'

'He'll be judged for his actions and then put in Praxos jail.'

'Praxos jail? Which one?' Emma asked, stepping closer to the thick glass that enclosed him.

'The one furthest from here I hope,' Lana replied.

'It depends on his sentence,' said Declan. 'But I'd imagine he'll be put pretty deep into the ground.'

'Deep into the ground? Huh?' asked Lana. 'What do you mean? Isn't it like a regular jail?'

Shaking his head, Declan headed towards the door. 'Nah, not for monsters like these. There's a place miles down from here. But you don't need to know about that. Not yet anyway,' he winked.

'Hey, how's Saleena?' asked Emma, glancing briefly at her sister.

'She's good, a bit better now that all this is over,' he smiled.

'What was wrong with her?' asked Lana slyly.

'I dunno,' he replied. 'Just tired, I guess.'

As he left the room, Lana winked at Emma and they giggled before turning their attention to Valentine who was still quivering in the corner.

'Hey, is he crying?' Emma asked quietly.

They both stepped closer to the glass and watched as the man's shoulders shuddered. The sound of soft sobbing could be heard.

'I guess so. That's what happens when you kill someone. The guilt consumes you, I suppose,' Lana said, but the moment she said it, she realised and gasped, looking over at Emma. 'Oh Sis, sorry I didn't mean to. I forgot...'

But Emma smiled and shook her head, 'Don't worry. You're right, the guilt can consume you if you've killed an innocent like Eleanor, not when you've killed an evil Skull like Sthenelaus. Don't worry, I'm fine now.'

'You...you... killed Sthenelaus?' asked the voice from within the glass cell.

Lana and Emma shared a worried look before Emma spoke.

'Yes I did. And you killed Eleanor.'

The man slowly lifted his head up from his knees and shook it.

'I didn't... I didn't kill her. That wasn't me,' he whispered.

'We know you did it, so don't give us this rubbish, Valentine.'

'But it's not true. I'm not a killer. Yes I worked for Madge, she forced me to. But I didn't kill anyone.'

Emma stole another glance at Lana who was avidly shaking her head.

'You don't actually believe this idiot do you? We saw him walk into that... that dungeon, where we found her dead, hanging... in chains... Emma.'

'Yes you're right,' whispered Emma as she turned to face him again. 'How do you explain that then?'

The man sobbed, 'It was her, not me. Madge did it. I was trying to... trying to... keep her alive. I didn't want her to die.'

'Go and get Declan back,' Emma whispered quietly to her sister. 'Oh, and perhaps it would be a good idea to get Penny as well.'

'Penny?' Lana asked.

Emma nodded, 'Opera et Veritate,' she whispered.

'Oh yeah of course,' Lana grinned. 'In action and truth. She can make him speak the truth. Emma, you're a genius.'

'I know,' she chuckled as Lana walked out of the room.

oOo

'Who are you?' asked Penny a little while later. 'What is your name?'

'I'm Valentine,' he said, sitting a little closer to the glass. His mask covering his eyes, keeping him in the dark.

'Your full name, Valentine?' she asked.

He nodded, twisting his fingers in his hands. 'Valentine Attwood.'

'Where are you from, Valentine?' Penny asked.

'Cornwall, England.'

'When were you born?'

'1775.'

Declan, who had been leaning back on his chair, suddenly let the chair fall forward. Penny gasped while Lana and Emma both stepped closer to her.

'1775?' Penny repeated.

'Yes that's right,' said the young man.

'Ask him how he got here,' Declan whispered into her ear.

'Valentine?' Penny asked.

'Yes, miss.'

'How did you get here, to our time?'

'Through the wormhole.'

'You can travel through time?'

'Only once.'

Declan looked at her and nodded, 'Just keep asking,' he mouthed.

Nodding, Penny continued with her questions, 'Only once? What do you mean? Can you tell us what happened?'

'Yes, Miss. I was just taking a Sunday morning stroll when I was summoned through the wormhole. I had no idea that it would bring me to this time and place so I stepped through. I just thought it would take me to another part of my county. But it didn't,' he said without taking a breath. 'When I came through it, I was surrounded by trees and there was the ocean. Only it looked very different from the ocean and the trees of home. It was then I realised I'd travelled further than I'd ever travelled before. Little did I know that I'd actually travelled through time.'

'Why did you stay, Valentine?'

'I couldn't go back.'

'What do you mean, you couldn't go back?'

'That woman stopped me from returning home. She said I must work for her before she would allow me to go home. She said I had to do everything she asked of me and then, when I'd finished my work, she'd let me go home,' he said, sobbing.

'Oh,' Penny said, looking at Declan.

'What work?' he asked directly to Valentine.

The young man lifted up his head and turned it sideways. He paused for a moment and then spoke. 'She had me digging graves, carving out trees, creating potions. And then, she asked me to transport her to different places. We came here once before when she... she hurt that woman.'

'Yes that's right. We saw you use your wormhole to transport a great deal of Skulls,' Emma said quietly. 'A few of us were injured that day.'

The man's sobs grew louder.

'Then what happened, Valentine?' asked Penny. 'What happened next?'

'We went to a place in the sea, like a ship of some kind. We stayed for a few hours before she asked me to transport her and a couple of others to Canada.'

'To Nova Scotia?' asked Declan.

Valentine shook his head, 'Not at first. First we went somewhere else. I believe it was called Alberta?'

Declan nodded. 'All sounds about right so far.'

'Was Eleanor with you all that time, Valentine?' Emma asked.

He nodded, 'Madge kept her close so she could create a spell.'

'The spell that made her look like Eleanor. She did the same with the man she'd been holding onto for years. She needed to use their blood and it had to be fresh,' he gulped loudly.

'Did you help her take the blood?' asked Lana.

But Valentine shook his head, 'No Miss. She wanted to do that herself.'

'And what happened when you were in Nova Scotia?'

'That's where I had to dig the graves and carve out the trees,' he cried.

'WHAT WERE THE GRAVES FOR, VALENTINE?'

'The Skulls she killed.'

'She killed her own people?' Lana gasped. 'Why?'

'She was testing the spell, the potion. It didn't always work,' he gulped again. 'They died.'

Lana and Emma looked at each other and shook their heads.

'I can't believe she would kill her own people for this,' Emma whispered.

'She didn't care,' Valentine cried quietly. 'All she cared about was killing you all. She wanted to kill all the Watchers in this world.'

'So all this time, you were just waiting for her to let you get back home?' Emma asked.

He nodded, 'But now I can never go back. Her secret has died with her. I will remain here forever,' he cried.

'Earlier you said that you were trying to keep Eleanor alive?' Emma asked. 'Why?'

'Because were it not for me, she would never have been taken in the first place. It was only because I could use my wormhole to get her into Praxos that this happened. Her blood was on my hands. I didn't kill her, but I might as well have done.'

Declan let out a deep sigh, 'He's just an innocent in all this.'

'He is definitely telling the truth,' Penny said, standing up and stretching her arms and legs. 'I have no doubt about that.

'So now what?' Emma asked. 'What are we going to do with him?'

Declan stood up and paced back and forth, rubbing his chin. 'There's only one thing we can do.'

The three girls all looked at him eagerly.

'We need to find out how we can send him home.'

On hearing this, Valentine's ears pricked and he sat up.

'You would... help me? After all this, you would help me find my way home?'

'Valentine, you're not to blame for this. Yes, you were forced to play her game but, ultimately, you're as innocent as we are. I believe you're actually a Watcher. Do you have a tattoo?'

'A tattoo? You mean, on my back?' Valentine asked.

Declan nodded, forgetting the man couldn't see him. 'Yeah mate, a tattoo on your lower back.

'Why yes, yes I do.'

'What does it look like?'

Valentine stood up and turned around, untucking his white shirt from his trousers and pulling it up to let them see.

All four of them gasped when they saw the most exquisite winged eye, much like their own but with even more detail. Stepping right up to the glass, Declan read the words beneath it, out loud, 'Historia Vitae Magistra'.

'Yes, yes that's right, Sir,' Valentine said, letting his shirt drop and turning to face them.

Declan walked to the back of the room and pressed a button on the wall. Immediately the glass walls began to lower into the ground.

'Valentine, you are a free man. I'm sorry we had to do this but we had no idea you were one of us.'

'I am... free? You are letting me go? But I don't understand? You say I am one of you?'

Stepping forwards, Declan lifted his hands towards Valentine's face.

'Declan!' Lana said loudly. 'Are you sure that's a good idea?'

'Lana, he's a Watcher. We have no right to keep him locked up.'

'He's right, Sis,' Emma reassured her. 'He's the victim here.'

'Yeah, I suppose you're right. Sorry,' she said to Valentine as Declan used the special tool to release the mask from his face.

As Valentine's eyes began to adjust to the light, he gently touched his face and turned to look at them.

'Thank you, I don't know what to say. Just that I am very, very sorry for the pain I have caused you and your people.'

'Our people?' Declan said. 'But you're one of our people now, Valentine. And it wasn't you that caused the pain. It was Madge. Like you said, you tried to keep Eleanor alive, right?'

Valentine nodded, 'Yes, yes I did. I tried to feed her but she didn't want it. When she was able to talk she told me to stop. She told me she wanted to die,' he cried.

'She did want to die, Valentine. It is what she wanted,' Emma sighed.

'Actually, it's what she needed,' Lana added. 'She's happy now though and that's what matters.'

'You... you have spoken to her?' he asked as they walked out of the room, and up some steep steps that led into one of the dark tunnels at the far end of the Praxos hall.

'Yes, she reached out to us after her death.'

'So she is at peace?' he asked.

'Very much so,' Lana smiled.

Content with the answer, Valentine smiled before they walked along the corridor that led into the great room.

Immediately, Valentine's expression changed and a cry escaped his lips.

'Look at the damage I have caused. I can't believe I was capable of this. How could I?' he cried, covering his face with his hands. 'I am an abomination. Take me back to the cell. I do not deserve freedom. I should be locked up forever.'

'Hey, hey calm down. No one was injured in the blast. While she was alive, perhaps her evil rubbed off on you a little bit. Plus, you thought you needed her to get home, Valentine. This was excessive of course, but you had a bloody good reason to do it. We forgive you, mate.'

'You do?'

Declan patted him on the shoulder and nodded.

'Well, I did place the explosives where I thought there would be few people. I didn't want to harm anyone, I just wanted a way to get in. You see, I couldn't use the wormhole to get in, only to get out.'

Declan nodded.

'I will do everything physically possible to help you clean this place up. What can I do, Sir?'

'First off, you can stop calling me sir. My name's Declan. Same goes for the girls. This is Penny, Lana and Emma. No Sir, Miss, Mrs or Ma'am or any of that. We are all equals here and in this day and age, we call each other by our names, got it?'

Valentine nodded shyly.

'And as far as cleaning this place up, we've got it sorted.'

'You have, Declan?' asked Lana, looking around at the mess.

'One of the Praxos Watchers has a particularly cool power that comes in handy sometimes,' he said glancing across the room. They soon spotted Wilbur standing in the middle, next to the Praxos statue, the marble child in his hands.

They watched his form change to one they had seen before, which had terrified them at first, but which was now all too familiar. As a Mothman, Wilbur was also capable of moving things without touching them.

First, the marble child lifted out of his hands, high up above him until it reached the arms of the Praxos woman. Carefully, the smaller statue seemed to find its place in her arms. Any cracks that had appeared during the blast and the subsequent crash with Madge, were simply erased. It was like the statue had never been harmed at all.

Slowly, other items within the room that had been crushed or destroyed, were miraculously put back together. Even the ceiling in the tunnel was returned to its prior place above them all. After about twenty minutes, the room looked immaculate, like there had never been an explosion at all.

'Why that's i...i...incredible,' Valentine stuttered.

The small group gave Wilbur a quiet applause before he disappeared into Eleanor's office to clean up the mess that had been caused in there.

'Eleanor's office,' Lana sighed, looking across the room.

'It's not Eleanor's office any more though is it?' Emma asked.

'It's Declan's,' Penny said as she walked away.

Emma had never seen so many people in one place before. The Academy was teeming with Watchers and humans, all dressed in bright colours, each one wearing a different shade from head to foot. Emma chose her favourite, purple, while Lana's outfit was entirely orange.

They were joined by their boyfriends, Barber dressed in red and Diarmuid in green. The girls laughed at the sight of them.

'It's weird seeing you out of jeans,' Emma smiled as he pulled her into his arms and kissed her gently on the lips. 'And all in green. You look like a leprechaun, a tall leprechaun,' she laughed.

'And you look like a beautiful healer,' he sighed, pulling her even closer and planting another kiss on the top of her head.

'Those two are so soppy,' Lana laughed as she linked arms with Barber and turned to look up at the Praxos statue.

'I still can't believe what happened.'

Barber beamed, 'I can. You kicked her ass and Praxos had the final word. Killed her with a Watcher child. If that's not karma, I don't know what is.'

Lana laughed, leaning into him. 'Praxos Karma, sounds good, babe.'

They were soon joined by the rest of their classmates, again each one wearing a different colour.

'This is the most bizarre funeral I've ever been to,' Liam said, feeling somewhat self-conscious in his green outfit.

'Hey, another leprechaun,' laughed Emma.

Liam snarled before cracking up and shaking his head. 'I suppose we do look a bit like that, don't we Diarmuid?'

'A cute leprechaun though,' Ava interrupted. She was dressed all in pale pink.

'Wow, you look amazing, Ava. Like a ballet dancer or something,' Emma grinned.

'A ballet dancer and a cute leprechaun?' Liam smirked. 'Can't get much better than that can we?' he joked as Declan appeared all dressed in white and stood on the pedestal above, just in front of the Praxos statue.

'Hey folks, can I have your attention please?'

As the noise died down, he continued, 'Thanks. Just quickly. Thank you to all of you for coming out on this occasion. We're not here to mourn the passing of our dearest friend and Guardian of the Fourth House of Praxos. We are here to celebrate her and to celebrate the life she had with us and it was a long one.'

Sounds of chuckling resounded throughout the room before he continued. 'Eleanor Hayden-Jones was one of the most incredible people I have ever had the pleasure of knowing. She was one of a kind. Always there when we needed her. Even in the face of tragedy, she always managed to look on the bright side of life,'

'Hey, isn't that a song?' yelled a voice from the crowd, adding to the lightness of the mood.

'Yes thanks for that Rupert,' Declan said before continuing. 'Eleanor was a light in the darkness, water when we were thirsty, and food when we were hungry. She was a trooper and we will all miss her terribly. But, she made me, and those soon to graduate, promise that we would not mourn her, that we would not be sad. We promised that we would celebrate her and be happy for her that she has finally found peace. Yes,' he said, nodding and looking around at the eager faces below, 'She finally found peace after hundreds and hundreds of years on this earth, she was able to move on with the love of her life, Tarquin,' he smiled. 'So let's hear it, everyone, let's hear it for Eleanor. Cheers Ellie,' he said. 'I'll miss ya mate,' he smiled before stepping down. 'Oh, one last thing,' he added, stepping back up. 'Day after tomorrow, it's classes as usual. Don't be late.'

Groans could be heard as well as laughter and a few sobs as the group began to disperse.

'Food and drink in the large dining hall people,' shouted a voice from the back of the room.

❧ 38 ❧

Missing his friends and family, Valentine sat quietly in the white room watching the multi-coloured dressed people mingle among one another while they mostly reminisced about Eleanor and the good she did for Praxos. He listened to stories about when she'd come down from above and met a man named Tarquin, before giving birth to a beautiful daughter, Marlene. Simply because she'd fallen in love and refused to return to the heavens, she'd been cursed with a half-life - ageing every day and becoming young again twelve hours later. Her daughter had been taken away from her and she'd watched as Tarquin aged and passed away, leaving her to live for the rest of her days alone.

Valentine listened intently, discovering the truth about the woman he'd tried to help while Madge did everything in her power to destroy her and everything Eleanor had built. A tragic story, one he felt terrible about being a part of. He wished he could've done things differently. He wished he could go back in time and stop it but it was impossible. He would probably never be able to travel in time again. He was probably destined to stay in this bizarre century until he died an old man.

Sighing loudly, Valentine turned his attention to a strange-looking chap, one with the body of a man and the head of a horse.

'Odd, isn't he?' said Emma as she approached and sat down beside him.

Valentine nodded and smiled as they both looked across the room at the creature who was leaning against the doorframe, nodding to the person next to him.

'He's a Tikbalang,' she said, offering him a bottle of water which he took with a smile.

'A Tikbalang? Strange name. What exactly is he?' he asked.

'He's also a shape shifter, can transform fully into a horse, which is how he gets around with the rest of the humans.'

'Oh,' Valentine nodded.

'His name is Dave,' she laughed.

Valentine chuckled, 'He doesn't look much like a Dave.'

'That's what most people say. How are you doing, Valentine?'

He shrugged and leaned back against the wall.

'Not so good?' she asked.

'I'm feeling a little... homesick,' he sighed.

'I can imagine. I wish there was something I could do to help.'

'Now that Madge is gone, I don't think it's possible. I guess I'm here to stay.'

'Not necessarily. Declan did say he wanted to help you, didn't he?' she asked gazing at him.

Valentine nodded.

'Well that means he'll do everything physically possible to help you get home. Declan's a really good guy. He always makes good on his promises. If there is a way for you to get home, we will find it. Don't you worry about that.'

'Thank you, Emma.'

'No problem,' she said holding up her bottle of water to his. 'Cheers.'

'Cheers.'

Sitting in silence for a few moments, they continued to watch the crowd of people change as they went in and out of the room, all chatting among themselves.

'Who is that?' asked Valentine as a beautiful young woman with long blonde hair wandered in, capturing almost everyone's attention. 'She looks familiar.'

'That's Marlene. Eleanor's daughter. She probably looks familiar because she does resemble her mother.'

'She certainly is beautiful,' he said, blushing when he realised Marlene was making a beeline for them.

Emma noticed out of the corner of her eye and smiled, standing up. Valentine immediately got to his feet too.

'Hey Emma,' she said before turning to him and asking, 'Valentine?'

'Yes, yes,' he muttered, a little embarrassed.

Marlene immediately grabbed him, pulling him towards her into a hug. Not quite knowing what to do, he lifted his arms and gently held her for a moment before she pulled back, holding him at arms length.

'I just wanted to thank you. For what you did for my mother. I heard you tried to help her. Tried to keep her alive. Thank you for being there for her when she needed someone. It means such a lot to me,' she said, the tears that had been welling up in her eyes, finally rolling down her cheeks.

'Oh, look at me. I'm a mess,' she sighed, gently rubbing her eyes.

'Here, allow me,' Valentine said politely as he delved into his pockets and pulled out a handkerchief. Very gently dabbing her cheeks with it, he looked deep into her eyes for a moment. Both of them blushed as he quickly looked away.

Emma, having watched the exchange, looked from one to the other and grinned before she silently stepped away, leaving Valentine and Marlene to get to know each other without her hanging around.

Walking through the room, she nodded, saying hello to the people she knew while others made a point of coming over to talk to her. They'd heard all about her healing skills and wanted to congratulate her on everything she'd done over recent weeks.

Embarrassed, Emma soon made her excuses and quickly walked out of the room straight into Declan.

'Oops, sorry, mate. You alright?' he asked.

Nodding, Emma smiled. 'Fine, fine. Nice speech earlier. How are you doing? Fully recovered yet?'

'Of course,' he said absent-mindedly rubbing his chest where the sword had stabbed him just a few days earlier. 'Never been stabbed and killed by a sword before. Not the best way to go, I can tell you,' he grinned. 'I'm looking for Valentine. You seen him?'

Emma pointed into the white room.

'I wouldn't interrupt him just yet though,' she grinned.

'No?' asked Declan.

'He's just met Marlene, look,' she said as they both leaned backwards, rather indiscreetly, to watch Marlene and Valentine who had clearly hit it off.

'Oh, nice,' he grinned. 'They look good together actually. Although, it's probably not the best idea.'

'What?'

'Getting it on with anybody right now. Not in this time anyway.'

'What do you mean, Declan?' she asked eagerly.

'I discovered something.'

Emma's eyes widened.

'About his time travelling,' he continued. 'I ought to really tell him. Come on, come with me. I really need to tell him before he gets too smitten.'

❈ 39 ❈

Sitting in the archives wondering what was going on, Valentine looked over at Declan who was holding a large book in his hands.

'I knew there was something familiar about your tattoo,' he said, 'So I started doing a bit of research of my own. It took a good few hours but eventually I found it. I found what I was looking for,' he said, handing the book to Valentine.

'What is it?' asked Emma, while Marlene peered over his shoulder.

'Those words, Historia Vitae Magistra. Look,' he pointed to the pages of the old book. 'They mean that history is life's teacher.'

'So?' asked Marlene, watching as Valentine pored over the book's words.

'I don't understand, Declan. What are you telling me?'

Declan grinned, 'You don't need us to help you go home. You can do it yourself.'

With his brows pinched together, Valentine shook his head, 'No, that's not possible. Madge was the only one that could do it. She was the one who summoned me here. She was the only that could send me back.'

'You're wrong, mate,' Declan said. 'Don't you get it? You're a Watcher, and no ordinary Watcher either. You have the power to travel through time. Didn't your father ever tell you?'

'My father?' Valentine queried.

'Yeah, mate. Your dad had the same talent.'

'But my father died when I was a child.'

'Oh, Valentine I'm so sorry,' Marlene said, placing her hand on his shoulder.

He looked up at her and nodded with a smile. Gingerly, he placed his own hand on top of hers. She almost jumped before biting her bottom lip.

Declan cleared his throat. 'What about your grandfather?'

'Yes, I was raised by my grandfather but he never mentioned this.'

'He was probably waiting for the right time,' Emma shook her head. 'There's never a right time though, is there?'

'So you're telling me that I already have the ability to travel home?'

Declan nodded, 'Not just home though. You are able to travel back and forth through time.

Historia Vitae Magistra - it's your job to make sure we don't forget our past. Not only are you a Watcher, but you're a Historian, mate. You're the one that ensures our future generations know what really happened in the past. You're pretty important to us Watchers, you know?'

'I am,' Valentine gulped. 'If it wasn't for you and your family, we wouldn't have all this,' Declan said as he turned around and pointed to the enormous archive.

'We did all this?' Valentine asked in awe.

'Yeah, mate,' he grinned.

'Wow,' Emma murmured. 'That's pretty cool.'

'It certainly is,' Marlene reiterated.

'But how?' Valentine stood up, slamming the book closed. 'I've never been able to jump through the wormhole to other times, only other places in the same time. I can't do that, Declan. It's impossible.'

But Declan patted him on the back. 'Nah, it's not, mate. You just need to train and learn how to control it. And I know just the person who can help.'

'You do?' asked Valentine. 'Who?'

'Yes, who, Declan?' asked Marlene.

'You Marlene. You possess many of the skills your mother had. You're the perfect candidate to help show Valentine the way home.'

Marlene immediately blushed and nodded. 'I guess I can try,' she said slowly.

'I have faith in you,' Emma added with a grin.

'When do we start?' Marlene asked as they all began to follow Declan out of the room.

'No time like the present,' Declan replied. 'But, you're going to need a place to start.'

'Right,' she replied. 'Where should we begin?'

'At the beginning?' Declan grinned. 'Right here,' he said, letting Emma walk through the doorway as he closed it behind them, leaving Marlene and Valentine alone.

'Do you really think that's a good idea?' Emma asked as they walked out into the corridor. 'They're clearly developing feelings for each other, Declan.'

'I know, but she's the best person for the job. This is the kind of thing Eleanor would've done in the past and, if Marlene is going to be a Guardian soon, she needs some practice herself.'

'Yeah you're right,' Emma sighed. 'I just hope it doesn't end in heartbreak, that's all.'

❧ 40 ❧

It had been three weeks since the funeral, and three weeks since Valentine had started learning how to hone his skills. Marlene was proving to be an amazing teacher, one he'd wished he'd had when he was younger, but his grandfather had chosen not to tell him the truth about their abilities and he did wonder why. He hoped, one day, to finally find out. But in the meantime, he had to work out how he would get back in the first place.

'That's fantastic,' Marlene said after he'd managed to go back a week and then return. 'How did it feel?' she asked.

'Good,' he said. 'But I've been thinking...'

'About what?' she asked, stopping what she was doing and looking up at him.

'If I can go back a few weeks, I could go back a few months and save your mother,' he blurted out.

'Oh,' Marlene said, taken aback. 'I hadn't even thought of that possibility, Valentine. It's a wonderful thought, really it is but...'

'But?'

Marlene shook her head, 'We cannot change what has already occurred. It would be so wrong to try and change the past. That is one of the most important things you must remember using your skill, Valentine.'

'I just thought...'

'I know,' she smiled sadly.

'I wanted to make you happy,' he blurted again.

'You did?' Marlene asked, her cheeks pinking slightly.

'Marlene, over these past few weeks, you have become so important to me. My feelings for you....' he stopped and stepped closer to her, '...have grown.'

Marlene stood up from the chair and gingerly stepped closer, before she stopped and turned away.

'I know,' she said, 'But...you will be leaving soon,' her voice broke.

'Do you feel it too, Marlene?'

She turned her head and nodded.

'Then come with me. I can take you through the wormhole when the time comes. We could make a life together back in my time.'

'I...I...I can't leave Praxos, Valentine. Praxos needs me. I need it,' she said quietly.

'I... understand, although I wish it wasn't the case. At least think about it. Take some time to really think about it... please,' he whispered, as he stepped even closer to her and pulled her into his arms.

Gazing up into his eyes, Marlene embraced him as he bent his head and very gently placed a soft kiss on her lips. The electricity between them both was almost visible.

oOo

'AND THEN HE KISSED ME,' MARLENE SIGHED, PLONKING HERSELF down on the bed next to Aria who was sitting up and sipping at a cup of mint tea.

'Oh wow, Marlene. That's so romantic,' she smiled. 'What are you going to do?'

'There is nothing I can do about it. He's from a different time, Aria. I can't go with him. It might change the past. We just don't know.'

'Marlene, are you forgetting where you've come from? You're from a different time too,' Aria laughed, almost choking on her tea.

'Careful,' Marlene said, taking the cup from her hands and placing it on the bedside table. 'You're still not fully recovered. Take it easy.'

Aria nodded, coughing into her hands.

'Well?' Aria asked.

'Well what?'

Aria's eyes grew wide with exasperation, 'You're from a whole other era too! Why not go back and live your life with Valentine?'

'What would you do, Aria?'

'There's no question, I would choose my man. Every. Single. Time. After losing John for a decade, there's no way I could ever be without him again. If you love him, truly love him, then you must go with him.'

Marlene looked away.

'Well?'

'Well what?' Marlene asked.

'Do you truly love him?'

Slowly, Marlene began to nod her head.

The door opened and before anyone appeared, a huge bunch of red roses made their appearance. John suddenly popped his head out from the side.

'Surprise,' he said. 'Oh sorry, I didn't know you had company.'

'It's okay John. I was just leaving. Lovely flowers,' Marlene smiled as she stood up.

'For my beautiful wife,' he grinned.

'I still can't believe you got married while she was in a hospital bed.'

'We just couldn't wait to spend the rest of our lives together,' Aria said from the bed, sitting up and brushing her hair back with her fingers. 'We'll have a proper celebration when I'm fully recovered.'

John put the flowers into a nearby vase before he leaned forward to kiss his new wife.

'You two are so cute,' Marlene said before she closed the door behind her. Sighing, she leaned against it for a moment before walking away.

❧ 41 ❧

Climbing off the motorbike and taking off the helmet, Lana placed it under her arm and waltzed over to her sister who was standing next to Barber as they'd watched her drive back down the road before pulling over.

'I can't believe you bought her a bike,' she sighed, shaking her head. 'And what's even more shocking is the fact that Mum and Dad approved.'

Lana laughed, 'Wanna come for a ride, Sis?'

'Nope, I don't think so,' she sighed, turning to go back into the Praxos Academy's main entrance.

'Aw c'mon Sis, don't be like that. It's great fun.'

'I'm sure it is. But you're the crazy one in the family. I'm quite happy to stay safe, thank you very much.'

'Stay safe? We're Watchers, we're always doing crazy stuff,' Lana smiled, following her through the main door, leaving Barber to cover the bike for her.

'All the more reason not to do some crazy stuff when we're not doing Watcher stuff,' Emma smiled, turning to gaze at her sister while she put the helmet down and took off her leather jacket.

'Well, I've wanted to be a biker for ages and now I am. I think it's cool,' Lana said, picking up the helmet and jacket.

'You think you're cool,' Emma smirked.

'I am cool. The cool sister, as opposed to the nerdy, goth sister,' she grinned.

'Hey!' Emma yelled at her before shrugging. 'For your information, I quite like being the nerdy, goth sister. Besides, it wouldn't do for us all to be the same.'

'I quite agree,' Lana laughed. 'So, what's going on, Sis? Why did you call us in this morning?'

'Because I have news.'

'News?'

Emma nodded, 'And I think you'll be quite excited about it.'

'Well then, do tell,' Lana waited.

'We've heard that's there's an opening at the Praxos Academy in Louisiana...'

'Yes?' Lana leaned in.

Emma chuckled, '... for an assistant to the Guardian and, apparently, they want you.'

'Me?' Lana breathed, taken aback. 'Why would they want me?'

'Why wouldn't they want you,' said a voice behind them, as Declan approached with a grin on his face.

'But I... I don't understand.'

Declan shook his head as Barber appeared.

'Come on, come into my office and we'll talk about it somewhere a bit quieter,' Declan said, turning away from the main door. Some students had just come out of a class and were starting to make rather a lot of noise.

'So, as Emma was saying,' Declan continued from behind the desk that once belonged to Eleanor, 'The Guardian of the New Orleans Academy has been watching you very closely over the past year, Lana and she wants you to go and work for her when you've finished your studies here in June.'

Lana gulped loudly. 'America?' she asked.

Declan and Emma laughed loudly. 'Louisiana is in America.'

'I'm going to live in America?'

'If you want to?' Declan asked.

The excitement on Lana's face suddenly drained and she turned to look at Barber who was looking a little forlorn.

'Oh, forgot to mention, they've invited Barber to come along too. They know you two are becoming quite the team.'

Lana squealed and jumped into Barber's arms. He caught her and laughed.

'But Em?' Lana suddenly said as Barber put her back on the ground. 'I've never left you before,' she whispered.

Emma looked sad, 'I know but I think it's time, don't you? We are eighteen now.'

Lana nodded, 'Yeah, I... er... I don't really know what it'll be like without you but I guess I should give it a try.'

'Give it a try. Lana, you're going to love it,' Declan smiled. 'The New Orleans Guardian has a pretty unique way of working and she travels, all the time.'

'Lots of travel?' Lana breathed. 'This sounds like the perfect job. I can't quite take it all in. Oh, but what about Mum and Dad? Surely they're not so happy about it.'

'Actually, I spoke with Patrick this morning and he's excited for you. Saddened that you'll be living so far away but he knew this day was coming. He's happy for you.'

'Really?' Lana breathed. 'I don't know what to say.'

'Well, just say yes so I can let her know,' he replied.

Lana, looking at all the expectant faces in the room, jumped up and down, 'Yes, yes, yes!' she squealed. 'I'm going to live in America.'

❧ 42 ❧

'I can't do it. I can't go,' Marlene muttered to herself as she looked in the mirror. 'I can't leave everyone I've grown fond of and just disappear into another time and place. I can't.'

'But he loves you,' said her own voice in her head. 'And you love him.'

But Marlene shook her head. 'But it's another time. How can I re-live that time again? I'll be changing the past and that's strictly against all the rules I abide by?'

'Marlene,' whispered a voice.

She turned around, looking around her bedroom, expecting to see someone standing there but it was empty.

Again, there it was, 'Marlene.'

'Who's there?' she asked, standing up and knocking the brush off the table onto the carpeted floor.

'Marlene, follow your heart, my darling. Follow your heart.'

'Mother?' Marlene whispered. 'Is that you?'

But her mother didn't appear.

'Mother?'

'Follow your heart, my darling, follow your heart.'

Turning to look around the room again, Marlene gasped at the sight of a woman walking away in the mirror.

'Mother, come back. Come back.'

The woman stopped briefly and turned to look at her daughter.

She smiled and nodded before disappearing into the depths of beyond.

'Follow your heart,' the words continued to sound in her head until eventually, all was silent.

Marlene slumped on the bed, pulling her hair into a side pony-tail and then dropping it so it hung loosely around her shoulders. Standing, she paced back and forth, before turning back to the mirror.

She sat staring into it for what seemed like ages, everything going back and forth in her mind. Eventually, she looked up and touched the mirror.

'Goodbye Mother,' she whispered before standing back up and walking towards the door. She opened it and quietly walked through, closing it behind her.

oOo

A GROUP HAD GATHERED AT THE FOOT OF THE PRAXOS STATUE where Valentine stood nervously. He was wearing a new outfit, something a local seamstress had created. She'd been told it was for a fancy dress party set in the early 1800s. Although it suited him, he looked very much out of place.

'I don't think she's coming,' he whispered under his breath.

'Are you ready, Valentine?' Declan asked. 'Are you ready to go home?'

Valentine looked down at him and furrowed his brow before nodding. He held a handkerchief in his hands that he continued to twist and his breathing was becoming louder and louder.

'Hey, mate. It's alright. You're going to do just fine. But you need to calm your breathing down a little bit. Alright?'

Valentine nodded but continued to twist the handkerchief.

'Are you ready?' Emma asked, Diarmuid standing closely beside her.

'Hey, I didn't miss anything, did I?' said a breathless Lana who had suddenly run down the corridor to get there. 'I didn't want to miss saying goodbye.'

'I'm still here,' Valentine smiled. 'Thank for coming, Miss Lana.'

'Miss?' she asked.

'If I am to return home, I must get back into the habit of conversing properly once again,' he said, nodding his head at her before he turned his attention to the growing group that had gathered to say goodbye.

'Firstly, my gratitude to you all for making me so incredibly welcome into your extraordinary lives. It has been such a pleasure to experience these past few weeks with you. The ones prior to that, not so much,' he said sadly. 'And I must offer my sincere apologies for being a part of such horrendous acts,' he bowed down.

'No need to apologise, Valentine. We've already talked about that,' Declan said, shaking his head.

Valentine nodded and continued. 'I shall never forget what you have all done for me. You are all truly selfless and remarkable friends and I shall miss you.'

'You could always come back,' Emma pointed out.

But Valentine shook his head, 'I'm afraid I shall have more pressing matters to attend to. After continuing my historical studies, it has come to my attention that the south western England from which I came, did - does - not have anywhere for Watchers to hone their skills, therefore I shall endeavour to create a Praxos Academy in Cornwall. I was rather hoping to take a certain someone with me to become the Guardian of said Academy but I fear she will not be...'

'Valentine,' said a voice from the darkened recess of the corridor.

Everyone turned, watching as Marlene appeared, walking quickly towards them.

'Marlene,' Valentine shouted, stumbling as he hopped down the step towards her. Seeing her dressed in an outfit to match his, he beamed. 'You will come with me?' he asked.

Taking his hands in hers, she nodded, 'I will. I will come with you.'

'Eleanor mentioned that Marlene was going to be a Guardian, remember, Sis?' Lana whispered, gently elbowing Emma in the ribs.

Emma nodded, smiling. 'Yep.'

Together, the duo climbed back up to the foot of the statue and turned to the crowd.

'She has chosen to join me in our quest,' Valentine said loudly, gently pulling Marlene's hand to his lips. 'Together we shall endeavour to do everything possible to help Watchers and humans alike.'

'And we will do our best to fight as many Skulls as possible too,' Marlene added with a grin.

The crowd erupted in cheers as Valentine chuckled.

'Are you ready, my love?' he asked.

Marlene nodded before she turned to look down at Declan. As the wormhole appeared before them, she placed her hand on her heart and mouthed, 'thank you'. And then she turned back to Valentine, who was holding out his hands to her. She took them, grinning and then, before everyone knew it, they'd gone, leaving behind only the echoes of their joyous cries, 'Stamus Contra Malum'.

$$\text{❦} \quad 43 \quad \text{❦}$$

Finally, life at the Praxos Academy was returning to normal. The students were busy studying for their finals, while Declan took to his new job as Guardian of the Fourth House of Praxos with gusto. Readying for the final exams, the place was quieter than usual. While most of Lana and Emma's classmates studied in the Archives, the younger students got their heads down, readying for their own yearly tests, which were coming up in a week or two.

Yawning loudly, Lana stretched her arms above her head, 'I could use a coffee,' she said, standing up and heading for the door. 'Can I get anyone else anything?'

A couple of people held up their hands while Diarmuid stood up and headed out with her, 'I could use a break', Diarmuid replied. 'I'll come and give you a hand. You coming, Emma?' he asked.

But she was glued to her book.

'Emma?' he asked again.

'Huh? What? Oh sorry,' she said, shaking her head. 'I'm good thanks. I'll stay here and carry on with this,' she said, holding the big book up. 'Maybe some water?'

She blinked a couple of times and rubbed her eyes, realising she'd been reading the same chapter over and over again.

Concentrating, she returned her attention to the book and continued on to the next chapter and immediately gasped.

'Oh My God,' she said under her breath and then again louder, 'Oh My God!'

'What? What is it?' said Sammy, from a few desks down. 'What's up?'

'This book, it mentions the Praxos Academy in Cornwall?'

'So?' asked Liam, looking up from the computer.

'It's about its creation. Look,' she pointed, reading out loud, 'The first Praxos Academy in south west England was created in 1801 by husband and wife Watchers Valentine and Marlene Attwood. The Academy was the first of its kind in Cornwall, offering food and board to anyone in need in the area. Its creators, and their four children, Declan, Barber, Emma and Lana, dedicated their lives to helping the needy, both supernatural and human and were known in the community for their depth of knowledge about everything historical. It is believed Valentine, Declan and Barber were, in fact, time travellers known for their painstaking efforts to transcribe all that had happened in the world for future generations to learn from...'

'Oh My God,' Sammy squealed. 'They named their children after you. That's so lovely.'

'Isn't it?' Emma sighed. 'I'm so happy it worked out for them. They deserved true happiness, those two.'

'But what happened to them?' Liam asked, leaning back in his chair. 'Marlene was immortal, wasn't she?'

'No, it says here they died within a month of each other in 1870. He was 95 years old, but it doesn't say how old she was. They had no record of her birth.'

'But how come she died if she was supposed to be immortal?' asked Sammy.

'I think she was only immortal while Eleanor lived. Once Eleanor died, the curse died with her.'

'That's kind of sad,' Sammy sighed.

'How could you think that? They lived a long, fruitful and happy life together. And then they died within a month of each other. That's true love,' Emma smiled as Diarmuid and Lana returned with trays containing hot mugs of coffee and bottles of water.

'What's true love?' asked Diarmuid. 'Are you talking about me again, Em?' he grinned.

'Of course,' Emma winked.

❧ 44 ❦

Several Months Later...

'So I guess this is it,' Emma cried, pulling Lana towards her and hugging her tight. 'I can't believe you're really leaving. I mean, it's amazing and everything but, well, you know. It's going to be so weird.'

Lana hugged her back. Neither of them wanted to let go.

'I know, Em. It's gonna be super weird, but we can handle it, can't we, Sis? We can Skype all the time, right?' she said, pulling back and looking at her sister.

'All the time,' Emma replied, wiping a few tears from her cheeks.

'Promise?' Lana asked, rubbing her nose.

Nodding, Emma pulled her sister close again for another hug, 'I promise.'

Eventually they released each other and stepped backwards. They stood looking at one another, both with trembling bottom lips.

'Come on, Lana. We ought to get going,' Barber said quietly.

'Barber, you better look after her,' Emma said as he hugged her a little too tight and she squealed quietly.

'Oh sorry, I forget my own strength sometimes,' he grinned, letting go. 'I promise I will take good care of her. You've got nothing to worry about.'

Emma nodded.

'Give my love to Mum and Dad, okay?' Emma said as she waved them off.

'We will, we'll be staying with them for a week before we head off to the States. It's still so weird when I say that,' she smiled as she climbed into the taxi.

'Promise you'll write,' Emma yelled. 'As well as Skype?'

'I promise,' Lana shouted through the open window as the car started to drive away. 'Love you, Sis,' she yelled.

'I love you too,' Emma yelled as loud as she could, stepping out onto the street as she waved, watching as Lana energetically waved through the back window of the London cab.

'Bye Lana,' Emma muttered before she turned back towards the door of Praxos.

'Hey,' Diarmuid whispered as he stood by the side of it. 'You okay?' he asked, watching as she wiped her eyes and nose with her sleeve.

She nodded but the tears began to fall and she shook her head.

'Hey, don't cry. We'll see her soon enough,' he reassured her, taking her into his arms.

'I...I...I'm just gonna... miss... her... so much,' Emma sobbed into his shoulder.

'I know, I know. Shhhhh,' he whispered.

As they walked slowly back into the main entrance, down the stairs and eventually reaching the main room, Declan walked up to them and smiled sadly.

'She's gone?' he asked.

Emma and Diarmuid nodded, as she wiped her nose again with her sleeve.

'Don't be sad, mate. She's gone to the States to do amazing things. She's going to be unbelievably happy, you know?'

'I...I know,' Emma eventually sighed.

'And you? Well, you're staying here to do great things too, right?' he asked.

Emma looked up at him and nodded, 'Yes I am,' she smiled, rubbing her eyes again.

'Well, let's start with this. I want you to run Praxos for a few weeks.'

'Huh? You want me to run Praxos?'

Declan grinned, 'Just for a couple of weeks while I... while Sal and I take a break.'

Emma beamed.

'Where are you going?' Diarmuid asked.

'Well, what with Sal's pregnancy and all, I decided she needs a bit of pampering, so I'm taking her home to India so her mother can spoil her before the baby comes.'

'But the baby's not coming for a while is it?' Emma asked, surprised.

'Actually, it's sooner than we thought,' he grinned.

'Sooner? How much sooner?' she asked.

'We have three months to plan everything,' his grin was insane.

'Saleena's having the baby in three months?'

Declan nodded.

'Wow.'

'Which is why we need a little break now before the little blighter arrives. So, will you do it? Will you look after Praxos while I'm away? You'll have plenty of help, of course. But, I just figured this would be good practise for you.'

'Good practise?' she queried.

'For the future. For when you become joint Guardian of the Fourth House of Praxos. My partner in crime.'

'Joint Guardian? Your partner in crime?' she grinned, remembering what Eleanor had told her. 'Declan, but I would be your assistant. Never for one second did I think I'd be your equal in all this.'

'My equal? Mate, you've been my equal for ages. Don't you realise how amazing you are? I don't want you to be my assistant, Emma. I want you to help me lead the Fourth House of Praxos. Are you ready for that?

'I... I can't believe it. Are you sure, Declan?'

'Of course I'm sure. It is what you want, right?'

Emma slowly nodded before jumping for joy. 'Oh yes, Declan,

it's exactly what I want. I can't quite believe it. Thank you so much for asking. While you're away, I promise that Praxos will be in good hands.'

'Oh I know, mate. I know. Praxos is going to be in the best hands possible. One of the Morgan Sisters. What more could I ask for?' Declan winked.

THE END

OTHER BOOKS IN THIS SERIES

Other books in the Praxos Academy series:
Daisy Madigan's Paradise
The Ghost of Josiah Grimshaw
The Temporal Stone
Looking for Lucy Jo

❧ 45 ☙

RAVEN 1

AN EXCERPT

The summer months were coming to an end when my parents disappeared. Although the day had begun like any other, it became one that I would never forget.

That morning, as usual, I sat at the kitchen table listening to the noises drifting up from outside - traffic, police sirens, people laughing and shouting - while I struggled to swallow the piece of dry bread that was shoved in front of me. "Eat," commanded my mother.

A small glass of milk just about helped it go down before she snatched the plastic tumbler from my hands, pulled me to my feet and shoved me out of the front door of our London flat without another word. Turning around to search her eyes, I attempted a smile in the hope that she might return it. But the door was shut in my face. A deep ache filled my stomach. I needed something that I had never experienced. I needed to know that she loved me.

Leaning against the door, I heard the familiar sound of her footsteps walking into the other room. She closed the door and locked it behind her. My mother and father had locked themselves in the spare room once again, just like they had done every day for as long as I could remember. I had always assumed they worked from home. I've no idea what they did, they never told me. I never asked. I wasn't allowed to ask questions.

Running down the four long flights of stairs, I pushed open the large heavy door that led outside. The noises multiplied and hit me, as did the dull smog and the intense London humidity that seemed to accompany every hot summer. As my feet touched the edge of the pavement, I stopped for a moment to allow a few cars to pass by before rushing across the road to school. I had to be quick. She was watching, she was always watching. My mother would peer down, staring blankly at me from the fourth floor window of the room she and my father spent their days. It was as if she was making sure I was actually going to school. Like I would dare do anything else. She never smiled. She never waved. She just stared. Sometimes it was almost as if she was looking right through me.

Returning home at lunchtime, as I was forced to do every day, she was there at that window staring at me again, as if her stare would physically guarantee that I came home. She had done it every day since I'd started school so it was normal to me.

I unlocked the front door with my key and gingerly tiptoed into the kitchen where I found her waiting for me.

"Eat and get back to school," she said with a glare as I perched myself onto the old metal stool and began spooning the cold soup into my mouth. It was the same cold soup I'd eaten every day. It would have been nice to have something else, a different flavour, perhaps, but I would never have asked. Oh no. I'd experienced my mother's anger one too many times before. It's not that she had ever hit me, but I knew. I just knew that she wanted to, so I avoided making her mad at all costs.

It was my belief that my mother's actions were the same as all other mothers. I imagined that she did what most mothers did. I didn't know any different. At least not until I met the newest girl at school, December Moon. When she had first arrived at the school, the other kids had sniggered and laughed when she had been introduced. Even I had thought it was a silly name to start with, but as soon as she spoke to me, I knew it was perfect.

After her introduction to the class, the only spare seat available was next to mine. As my fellow students were in the habit of ignoring me, I was a little startled to have this pale but pretty flame-haired girl smile at me as she approached and sat down. I shyly returned the smile as she quietly took out her books and a pencil case from the orange rucksack she had carried on her back. Her clothes were multi-coloured and flowing – a long heavy purple flowery skirt was paired with an orange and pink striped top, and brown boots. A brown headband held back her straight shoulder length hair and when she turned I noticed it had a pink flower sewn onto it. Ordinarily, the colours wouldn't work together but on December, they just seemed to fit... perfectly.

When the attention was no longer on her, December turned to me and whispered "hello". She smiled again and her whole face changed. It lit up.

It didn't take long for December and I to become best friends. We were both shy and quiet and were mostly ignored by everybody else. It made sense that we should spend school time together. More than anything though, I wanted to be friends out of school hours. My mother, however, had always made it quite clear that friends of any kind were strictly forbidden. Fortunately, she couldn't see past the school gates, so December always waited for me inside, out of mother's view. She was my secret.

December and I had spent many a break time chatting about each other's lives. She was an avid reader of all kinds of books, even magazines. In fact reading was pretty much all she did when she was at home. I was in awe of her and I knew then that she must know a lot more about other people's lives than I did. That was how I learned that my parent's actions were not entirely normal. Her own parents, however, could not be described as 'normal' either.

"My father died when I was three," she had told me soon after we'd met. "He was a very old man and I was very young so I don't remember him."

The edges of my mouth turned downwards as the heavy feeling of sadness took effect. "And what about your mother, December? Where is she?"

"She dumped me with my father's family shortly after he died and moved back to America on her own. She was from Seattle, Washington, apparently." Her response was so matter-of-fact that I didn't quite know what to say, other than "Oh."

"Basically, my Aunt Penelope – that's my father's younger sister who I live with – tells me that my mother married my father for his money but when he died, leaving her with nothing, she dumped me with her and took off."

"Aunt Penelope basically makes sure I am fed, schooled and clothed. Other than that, we don't have much time for each other." She shrugged her shoulders. "But that's fine with me. She doesn't like to be seen with me, especially when her super rich friends are around. Being my mother's daughter lowers the tone of her family... I even heard her say that to Monty once. Oh, Monty's our butler, chauffeur and sometimes gardener," she shrugged again and that's when I saw a glimmer of something in her eyes. She wasn't quite so emotionless about it all after all.

Having never known anyone rich before... and with a butler too, I thought it was quite weird for her to be a student in the same school as me. "December?"

"Hmm?"

"Why doesn't your Aunt Penelope send you to a posh school?"

"Like I said, she'd rather I didn't exist so she'd rather keep me as far from her friends as possible."

"That makes sense, I guess. In which case, I'm glad! I would never have met you otherwise! So do you not know anything about your mother?" I asked, intrigued.

December shook her head, "Nope. Nothing."

The sound of the school bell put an end to our conversation and December didn't mention her mother or her father to me again for a very long time.

Discreetly waving goodbye to her on that fateful day, I knew there was something wrong the moment I stepped foot out of the school grounds. Looking up to the window expecting to see mother, a vision in white as usual, there was no sign of her. My heart began to thud faster in my chest as I ran as fast as I could up the stairs two at a time. I grappled with the key and pushed open the front door. She was nowhere to be seen. Neither was my father.

46

RAVEN 2

The spare room was locked as it always was, and no matter how hard I banged my fists on that door, there was no reply. I stopped and put my ear carefully against the solid wood to check for any sounds but there was nothing. Just silence. Trying to kick the door down, I didn't even leave a single mark. I was just a slight girl with little strength, after all.

It was then that our neighbours, Dorothy and June, came rushing in.

"Oh my dear, my dear! Whatever is the matter? What is all this banging about?" yelled one of the sisters as they tried to calm me down.

"It's mother," I said, "she's... she's disappeared. She's always here. I don't know what's happening. There's no answer at the door. Something's wrong," I sobbed.

Just at that moment, the sisters' black cat wandered in behind them. It immediately began purring at my feet and rubbed itself against my legs. It had never set foot in our apartment before and it was strange that it did so then.

It jumped up so that it balanced on its hind legs and leaned against me. I momentarily forgot all about the commotion that I had caused and leaned forward to pick it up, cuddling it while it continued to purr. "That's strange," said June, "she's usually terrified of people." The cat was clearly not terrified of me. It was the first time I had ever stroked an animal and I felt a strange affinity with it. It was a wonderful feeling as it rubbed its head against my neck. Looking into her deep, warm eyes, for a moment I felt a strange sensation within me. It felt as though I was being loved. I didn't want to lose the feeling so I sat down on the floor and stroked her soft fur, smiling.

"I'm going to call the police," one of the sisters said as the other tried to coax me off the floor. I didn't feel myself, for some reason. A strange trance-like state came over me.

"Come now, dear. Come and sit on the sofa. You'll catch your death on those cold floor tiles."

I did as I was told and followed her to our uncomfortable hard red leather sofa, where we waited until the police arrived. The cat sat on my lap and the two sisters sat on either side of me.

"We know that your mother leads a strict routine, my dear, so to hear you banging on the door like that had us worried," said June.

"We've never known anything ever happen to you like this so we thought we'd better come over straight away and find out what's going on," added Dorothy as she gently patted my hand with her own wrinkled, yet perfectly manicured, fingers.

My calm moments with the cat were cut short by the arrival of two young uniformed male police officers, followed by a third woman. The cat jumped out of my arms like a shot. She was clearly spooked by the presence of strangers and had vanished from our flat, presumably to return to the safety of her home. My calm feeling faded the moment she was gone.

The female police officer was very kind and polite and asked me a few questions about myself and my parents. When had I last seen them? Where did they work? Was it common for them to leave without telling me? Did they have mobile phones? I didn't even know the answer to the last question, although if they did, I never saw or heard them. Technology wasn't a word I heard used in our home. Not that there were ever many words used at all.

More questions were asked of me and so I answered them as best as I could before the other two police officers managed to literally knock the door down. I wasn't prepared for what I saw and

I don't think they were either. There was almost nothing. Just a simple room, painted black – the floors, ceiling and walls all painted black. There were no chairs, no desks, nothing. The only things to be seen in the room were a small black shelf which contained two glass vials. One was filled with a thick deep red liquid and the other contained what appeared to be something from the insides of an animal – I couldn't identify it, but it looked disgusting. A pang of fear shot through me. Fear for my parents' safety.

"Do you have any idea what substance this is, Miss?" asked one of the police officers.

I shook my head. "I've never been in here before."

The two men gave each other a sideways glance that was way too obvious for me not to have seen.

"Right then, Miss, would you like to wait outside while we gather some of this evidence together?" said the first officer as the other led me out of the black room.

Snippets of conversation could be heard as I waited for them to finish.

"This is definitely blood. What on earth do you think has been going on in here then, Pete?"

"Beats me, Dave. I tell you one thing though, it's weird, whatever it is. It's almost like something out of a horror film. Here... look at this."

The female officer appeared by my side and cleared her throat. The conversation in the black room suddenly became quieter.

"Don't worry, Lilly. We'll get to the bottom of this," she said, smiling. "We'll find your mum and dad."

After about half an hour, the officers appeared from the room, carrying the vials in two clear plastic bags.

"Okay, Constable Madley, we've all the evidence now. We'll take them to the lab for tests," said the taller of the two.

He tipped his hat to me and smiled before carrying everything out of the flat.

Following behind, the other one stopped in front of me and crouched down, looking right into my eyes. His dark brown eyes and the soft laughter lines around his mouth gave him a look of kindness. I hadn't noticed when they'd first arrived. "Lilly, we'll be in touch as soon as we have any information as to the whereabouts of your parents. Don't worry. We'll find them." He stood up then and patted Constable Madley on the back. They were clearly friends as well as colleagues. He smiled at her, "Thank you, Constable Madley. We'll see you back at the station."

❧ 47 ❧

RAVEN ₃

My parents' disappearance continued to be a complete mystery. The police had told me that even though they had followed several lines of enquiry and spoken to countless people; they had come up without a single clue to go on. Not one person had seen them. I was the only one that had seen them that day. Well, I had seen her. I hadn't actually seen my father. I had just assumed he was there. I rarely saw him anyway, I rarely even heard him. Every now and then I would hear her speak to him but I never heard him reply.

It had been a hot and humid summer and, unusual for England at that time of year, it had lasted for quite a few weeks. Naturally, there had been a hose pipe ban as happened every time the sun shone for more than a week there. I had only been aware of it because my teachers were keen to teach us all about current environmental issues.

Not that I noticed the ban. We didn't have a garden, we didn't even have any plants. Our home was a bare flat in London where I had lived all my life – all thirteen years of it. I can't say I was happy, nor can I say I was particularly unhappy because I wouldn't have known the true meaning of either word.

I was very much a loner with no friends until December came along. Luckily, the majority of kids at school were pleasant enough to us but we didn't feel like we belonged with any of them so we simply avoided contact. Of course there were a few that taunted us every now and again, but we took little notice. They seemed to taunt a lot of people at school, having silly nicknames for everyone - apart from December. The kids were amused enough by her name not to bother making up another. Mine was Mellow Yellow – probably because I was so quiet and wore a lot of yellow. Not by choice though. The few clothes that I owned were bought by my mother and for some reason they were all yellow, not even a nice shade of yellow. All were second-hand clothes and none fitted me properly, but I certainly couldn't complain even if I hated them all. Like I said, my parents and I didn't really talk.

December and I preferred being in our own little world, alone with our thoughts or curled up with a sneaky book under the large chestnut tree in the playground.

At school, we blended into the background. We were courteous to most people and most of them were courteous to us. Yet if you asked anyone about me, even my name, I doubted very much that any of the kids would know. At least that was the case until my parents mysteriously vanished from the face of the earth. Then everyone seemed to know my name. Everyone knew I was Lilly Taylor.

Word had spread rapidly as I walked through the school gates a few days later.

Out of habit, December had waited hidden behind the walls for my arrival. She needn't have, of course. She hugged me tightly but didn't say a word. Somehow she just knew how I felt.

Shame the other kids didn't have a clue. Fingers pointed, people whispered and stared at me. Not a single other person approached me. Had it not been for December, I would have felt even more alone than I had ever felt before. I could easily have cried on her shoulder but the tears did not come. As much as I wished they would, they wouldn't come, perhaps because I had never really had much of a relationship with either parent. I never felt loved. I never even felt liked. But they were my family.

The closest people to me at that time of my life, other than December, were the kind neighbours who had offered to take care of me until my parents were found. Or, in the event that they did not return, until plans were made for me to travel across the world to stay with my grand-father in Canada. A grand-father I knew nothing about. December would be crushed. I was her only friend and she needed me as much as I needed her. I would hate to have to leave her, but deep down I knew that it was likely.

Rather than put me into temporary foster care, Social Services had agreed that my staying with the sisters was the best thing for me. Familiarity, they said, would be better than handing me over to complete strangers. Dorothy and June were spinsters. They had never married but had been happy enough living together their entire lives. They were good and honest and they were trustworthy. I couldn't really have stayed with December even if I had wanted to. She didn't have the best relationship with her aunt. What her wealthy aunt gave to December in financial security, she lacked in love. She was as lonely as I was and her aunt would never have allowed her to take me home with her.

Later that afternoon, I had rushed out of the school gates and looked up at the window to see if my mother had come back. She wasn't there, of course. No vision in white.

As I stood there, it occurred to me that for the very first time in my life I could do anything I wanted. Anything in the world. But I had no idea what to do. I looked around and watched many of the other kids laughing and joking. Some kicked around a football, others sat on the wall sneakily smoking cigarettes, while some of the younger ones were collected by their loving parents. December sadly waved goodbye from her chauffeur-driven car.

Instead of heading 'home', I gingerly walked in the opposite direction, looking back over my shoulder afraid that someone might swoop down and pull me back. Yet for the first time ever I felt no pull to return to that place. If it wasn't for Dorothy and June, I would probably have just carried on walking, but deep down I knew I couldn't hurt them like that. Especially when they had shown nothing but kindness to me.

So I turned around and headed back up those stairs. The ones I had walked up a million times before. Yet this time, I entered the apartment across the hall from my parents' place. As I unlocked the door, the most delicious smell of home cooking invaded my every pore and the sounds of laughter came from the living room. I followed the sounds and instead of finding the sisters, I found the television switched on. I sat down and watched for a few minutes, laughing at the silly man who pranced around like a complete idiot getting himself stuck in silly situations. Watching until it finished, I discovered that he was called Mr Bean. It was then that I felt an overwhelming sense of guilt for doing something I was never permitted to do. I peered over my shoulder guiltily before getting up and walking into the kitchen.

"Oh hello, dear. You're just in time for dinner. Come in. Don't just hover by the door. I hope you had a good day at school. I've made us a Shepherd's Pie. I hope you like that," said Dorothy as she gently pushed her white blonde curls behind her ears before spooning the food onto a plate for me.

I had no idea what a Shepherd's Pie was, but I nodded enthusiastically nonetheless. It was easily the most delicious meal I had ever had. At home, everything came straight from a tin. Tinned spaghetti, tinned beans, tinned peas, tinned mince, tinned potatoes, tinned soup, and so on. And most of it was given to me cold. Stone cold. I only knew it was all tinned food because of the time I had sneaked in when she wasn't looking and had opened the cupboards to find a lifetime's supply of the stuff.

I had never been allowed to spend any length of time in our kitchen, other than to quickly eat, so I had no idea how to prepare food. I guess back then I had assumed that everybody ate that kind of stuff.

"Did this come out of a tin, Dorothy?" I asked.

"Oh my dear!" she said, "Of course not. We cook everything fresh in this house. Did your mother never prepare you a home cooked meal?"

I shook my head and told her about the kinds of things I had eaten and she looked shocked, as did June.

"I take it that means she never taught you to how to cook?"

I shook my head again and told them I wasn't allowed in the kitchen other than to quickly eat.

"Well, while you're staying with us, we'll just have to change that, won't we? We'll show you everything you need to know. But first, eat up and enjoy dear. We'll start to teach the basics tomorrow after school," Dorothy smiled kindly as she patted my hand.

As I enjoyed those wonderful mashed potatoes with the tasty meat beneath, I felt another pang of guilt. Guilt that my parents had vanished and there I was, stuffing myself like some sort of famished orphan. But then, perhaps that's what I had become. An orphan. And I was hungry. Very hungry.

That evening, the guilt continued to consume me. So much so that I felt the need to do something about it. Something drastic. And there was only one thing that I could do. I secretly borrowed a pair of scissors from the kitchen and sneaked into the bathroom. After locking the door, I stood looking at my reflection in the mirror and before I could talk myself out of it, I took those scissors to my hair and hacked it all off. As I stared at myself, I wished for that guilt to disappear. It didn't. I needed to do more. Searching through the sisters' belongings in the cupboard, I came across a box with a picture of a woman with the same coloured hair as Dorothy. Without giving it a second thought, I opened the box, emptied the contents on the floor and sat on the bath mat as I read everything on the leaflet inside the box. As instructed, I mixed the contents of the bottles together and began covering my hair with the cream. The strong odour made my eyes water as I slowly began to bleach out the black from my hair.

Over an hour later, I stood staring at my reflection, a mountain of long black hair covered the floor by my feet. I inched closer to the mirror and stared into my eyes. Their usual shade of vivid green seemed flat and lifeless. Murky. I wished the guilt would disappear. I wished for tears to come. I wished for the return of my parents. But it was no good. There was no one to make my wishes come true.

I crept back into the spare bedroom and pulled out all of my awful yellow clothes. Spreading them on the soft pink carpet, I used the same pair of scissors to cut them and rip them so that they didn't hang loosely from my body any more. Just for a moment, I forgot my circumstances and enjoyed the creativity. What I was left with, however, wasn't what I had intended. They were still a mess, and they were all still yellow. I didn't want to wear yellow any more. I didn't want to be the Mellow Yellow girl.

I walked into the living room where Dorothy and June sat glued to the television, and I stopped in the doorway to watch the screen for a few moments. I listened as a middle-aged man talked about a recent spate of mysterious attacks on horses that had taken place within the London area.

A minute later, the cat jumped off the sofa and started making a fuss of me. The two women noticed and turned to see what she was so interested in. Dorothy let out a cry when she saw me. June gave me a hug. She just seemed to understand why I had done it. I sat down in between them both on the sofa and told them what I had done to all my clothes. Their look of sadness didn't go unnoticed by me and I felt bad for making them feel that way.

As the cat rubbed itself against my bare legs, Dorothy suddenly stood up and smiled with a twinkle in her.

"I have an idea," she said, "come on."

June stood up too and laughed, "Of course."

"We always wondered why your mother dressed you in yellow, dear. It's really not a flattering colour for you at all. I know we're just a couple of old spinsters, but we've still got our clothes from when we were younger. We just might have some things that will fit you. Let's go and have a look," added June.

I followed the sisters into a fourth bedroom, a room without a bed, instead filled with hangers and hangers of clothes. I had never seen so many bright and beautiful things. It wasn't just the colours that were so beautiful to me, it was the feel of the clothes, soft and silky. So unlike the hard and scratchy fabrics I had always worn.

However, as much as they tried to give me colourful skirts and blouses, I found myself drawn to black. With my newly-dyed white hair, I told them I just wanted to wear black. Deep down, I felt unworthy somehow of wearing anything else. Eventually they conceded and pulled out everything they had in black. There wasn't much but it was a far cry from Mellow Yellow. That night, the sisters' sewing machine went into overdrive – making all my new clothes to fit my small frame.

Walking through the school gates the following day I held my head up high and let them point and stare. There were whispers but there were also wolf whistles from the heartless boys that didn't care for my emotions. But I couldn't care less. Nobody called me Mellow Yellow after that. I was finally just Lilly.

"Your hair!" were the first words from December's mouth. "As much as I loved the black hair, I do love the white, although I'm not so keen on the hacked look," she giggled. December was always good at making me feel better with a well-timed, and much-needed joke. She didn't mention my missing parents or the lack of yellow. She didn't need to. She was just there and that was all that mattered.

As the weeks went by without any sign of my parents, true to their word, Dorothy and June began to demonstrate how to cook all kinds of simple recipes. They tried to keep me busy. The police concluded that the blood they had found was my father's, but they neglected to tell me what was in the other vial. However, as they had made no further discoveries, it looked as though the case may well be shelved, unsolved. An X file. I didn't know what to think. A vial of my father's blood? Did that mean he was injured? Or worse? I tried not to let my imagination run wild.

From conversations with the Social Services, the authorities and Dorothy and June, I knew I would have to move to Canada. My grand-father telephoned me and told me that all the arrangements had been made. We didn't have much to say to each other. Not just because I didn't know the man, but also because I simply wasn't used to talking on the telephone.

In just a few short weeks, I would no longer live in England. A sense of sadness overcame me but still the tears did not come. I was upset that I was leaving my parents behind... wherever they were. But it was the fact that my life had actually improved since they'd disappeared that made me feel guilty. The guilt turned to sadness and the sadness turned to guilt, like an unstoppable swinging pendulum.

RAVEN IS AVAILABLE FROM MOST ONLINE BOOK RETAILERS

ABOUT THE AUTHOR

Suzy Turner wrote her first chick lit novel in her early twenties, but it wasn't until much later that she decided to focus on writing full time. It was during a visit to Canada in 2009 when the ravens within the dark eerie forests of British Columbia called to her. The story of Lilly Taylor was born soon after and the first novel in The Raven Witch Saga was created. Suzy has since published several more urban fantasy books (under her pen name SG Turner) and contemporary women's novels.

Having lived in Portugal since childhood, Suzy, who is originally from Yorkshire in England, loves to travel. She finds inspiration wherever she goes. Old decrepit buildings, graveyards, cathedrals and castles are just a few of the things that can be found within the worlds of her urban fantasy books, and her contemporary women's fiction novels are filled with fun friendships, ordinary people in extraordinary circumstances and quirky characters you'd want as friends.

Suzy lives in the Algarve with her husband, three cats and a dog, where she does yoga every morning and bookish stuff for pretty much the rest of the day!

For more books and updates, visit www.suzyturner.com or www.chilloutpress.com

facebook.com/sgturnerbooks

twitter.com/suzy_turner

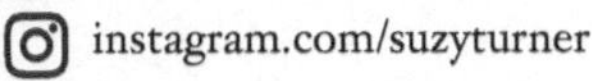
instagram.com/suzyturner

ACKNOWLEDGMENTS

ACKNOWLEDGEMENTS

Huge thanks to my amazing beta readers who never fail to make me smile with their positive comments about my work. They are simply amazing.
And of course, to my amazing readers for your continued support. I couldn't do it without you.

* 9 7 8 9 8 9 5 4 6 4 8 0 7 *